# NOT JUST
## A WITCH

Eva Ibbotson was born in Vienna, but when the Nazis came to power her family fled to England and she was sent to boarding school. She became a writer while bringing up her four children, and her bestselling novels have been published around the world. Her books have also won and been shortlisted for many prizes. *The Secret of Platform 13* was shortlisted for the Smarties Prize, and *Which Witch?* was runner-up for the Carnegie Medal. *The Ogre of Oglefort* was shortlisted for the Guardian Children's Fiction Prize and the Roald Dahl Funny Prize. Eva Ibbotson died peacefully in October 2010 at the age of eighty-five.

*Books by Eva Ibbotson*

The Beasts of Clawstone Castle
Dial A Ghost
The Great Ghost Rescue
The Haunting of Hiram
Monster Mission
Not Just a Witch
The Ogre of Oglefort
The Secret of Platform 13
Which Witch?

Let Sleeping Sea-Monsters Lie . . .
and Other Cautionary Tales

The Dragonfly Pool
Journey to the River Sea
The Star of Kazan

*For older readers*
A Company of Swans
Magic Flutes
The Morning Gift
The Secret Countess
A Song for Summer

# NOT JUST A WITCH

# EVA IBBOTSON

MACMILLAN CHILDREN'S BOOKS

First published 1989 by Macmillan Children's Books

This edition published 2015 by Macmillan Children's Books
an imprint of Pan Macmillan
20 New Wharf Road, London N1 9RR
Associated companies throughout the world
www.panmacmillan.com

ISBN 978-1-4472-6570-2

3 5 7 9 8 6 4 2

A CIP catalogue record for this book is available from
the British Library.

Typeset by Intype Libra Ltd
Printed and bound by CPI Group (UK) Ltd, Croydon CR0 4YY

*For Bertie, Freddie, Theo
and Octavia*

# Chapter One

When people quarrel it is bad, but when witches quarrel it is terrible.

Heckie was an animal witch. This didn't mean of course that she was a witch who was an animal; it meant that she did animal magic. Her full name was Hecate Tenbury-Smith and she had started when she was still a child, turning the boring noses of her mother's friends into interesting whiskery snouts or covering the cold ears of traffic wardens with thick black fur. She was a kind girl and only wanted to be helpful, but when she gave the swimming bath attendant red spots and a fishy tail so that he could pretend to be a trout if he wanted to, her parents sent her away to a well-known school for witches.

It was a school for making *good* witches. The motto the girls wore on their blazers said WITCHES AGAINST WICKEDNESS and the headmistress was choosy about whom she took.

Heckie was very happy there. She made a lot of friends, but her best friend was a stone witch called Dora Mayberry. Dora wasn't *made* of stone, but she could turn anything *into* stone. When Dora was still in her high chair, she had looked at a raspberry jelly out of her round little eyes and it turned into something you couldn't cut up even with a carving knife. And when she started turning the toothpaste

1

solid in its tube and filling the fridge with statues of pork chops, she too was sent away to school.

It takes thirty years to train a witch and during all that time, Heckie and Dora were friends. Heckie was tall and thin with frizzy hair, pop eyes and teeth which stuck out, giving her an eager look. Dora was squat and solid and had muscles like a footballer because it is heavy work dealing in stone. They shared their secrets and got each other out of scrapes, and at night in the dormitory they talked about how they were going to use their magic to make the world a better place.

By this time Heckie could change any person into whatever animal she pleased by touching him with her Knuckle of Power (though for the best results she liked to use her Toe of Transformation also) and Dora could turn anybody into stone by squinting at him out of her small round eyes. And then, when they had been friends for thirty years, Heckie and Dora quarrelled.

It happened at the Graduation Party where all the witches were to get their diplomas and get ready to go out into the world. The party, of course, was very special, and both Heckie and Dora went separately to the hat shop kept by a milliner witch and ordered hats.

Obviously a witch on the most important day of her life is not going to turn up in a straw hat trimmed with daisies or a bonnet threaded with sky-blue lace. Heckie thought for a long time and then she ordered a hat made of living snakes.

The snakes were mixed. The crown of the hat was made of Ribbon Snakes most delicately woven;

2

edging the brim were King Snakes striped in red and black and a single Black Mamba, coiled in the shape of a bow, hung low over Heckie's forehead.

Heckie tried it on and it looked lovely. The snakes hissed and spat and shimmered; the flickering tongues made the hat marvellously alive. Snake hats are not only beautiful, they are useful: when you take them off you just put them in a tank and feed them a few dead mice and a boiled egg or two and they last for years.

The day of the party came. Heckie put on her batskin robe, fixed a bunch of black whiskers on to her chin – and lowered the hat carefully on to her curls. Then she set off across the lawn to the tent where the refreshments were.

But what should happen then? Coming towards her was her friend Dora – and she was wearing exactly the same hat!

It wasn't roughly the same. It was exactly the same. The same Ribbon Snakes heaving and hissing on the crown; the same King Snakes writhing round the brim; the same poisonous Mamba tied into a bow!

The two witches stopped dead and glared at each other and the other witches stood round to see what would happen.

'How dare you copy my hat?' cried Heckie. She was really dreadfully upset. How could Dora, who was her best friend, hurt her like this?

But Dora was just as upset. 'How dare *you* copy *my* hat?' she roared, sticking out her jaw.

'I chose this hat first. I am an animal witch. It is my *right* to wear a hat of living snakes.'

3

'Oh, really? I suppose you've heard of my great-great-great-grandmother who was a Gorgon and had serpents growing from her scalp? It is *my* right to wear living snakes.'

But showing off about your relatives never works. Heckie only became angrier. 'The only thing you've got a right to wear on your head is a bucket,' she shrieked.

This was how the quarrel started, but soon the witches were throwing all sorts of insults at each other. They brought up old grudges: the time Dora had turned Heckie's hot-water bottle to cement so that Heckie woke up with her stomach completely squashed. The time Heckie borrowed three warts from Dora's make-up box and got cocoa on them . . .

From shouting at each other, the witches went on to tug at each other's hats. Dora tugged a Ribbon Snake out of Heckie's brim and hung it on a laurel bush. Heckie pulled at the end of Dora's Black Mamba and undid the bow. And all the time they screamed at each other as though they were spoilt little brats, not respectable middle-aged witches.

Ten minutes later both their hats were in ruins and a friendship which had lasted all their school-days was over.

The witches had planned to go and live close together in the same town. They were each going to buy a business where they could earn their living like ordinary ladies, but all their spare time would be spent in Doing Good.

Now Heckie went by herself to the town of Wellbridge, but Dora went off to a different town.

It was without her best friend, therefore, that Heckie began to try and make the world a better place.

# Chapter Two

It was a boy called Daniel who found out that a witch had come to live in Wellbridge.

He found out the night he went to babysit for Mr and Mrs Boothroyd at The Towers. Mr Boothroyd owned a factory on the edge of the town which made bath plugs and he was very rich. Unfortunately he was also very mean and so was his wife. As for his baby, which was called Basil, it was quite the most unpleasant baby you could imagine. Most babies have *something* about them which is all right. The ones that look like shrivelled chimpanzees often have nice fingernails; the ones that look like half-baked buns often smile very sweetly. But Basil was an out and out disaster. When Basil wasn't screaming he was kicking; when he wasn't kicking he was throwing up his food and when he wasn't doing that he was holding his breath and turning blue.

Daniel was really too young to babysit and so was Sumi who was his friend. But Sumi, whose parents had come over from India to run the grocery shop in the street behind Daniel's house, was so sensible and so used to minding her three little brothers that the Boothroyds knew she would be fit to look after Basil while they went to the Town Hall to have dinner with the Lord Mayor. What's more, they knew they would have to pay her much less than they would have to pay a grown-up for looking after their son.

And Sumi had suggested that Daniel came along. 'I'll ask you your spellings,' she said, because she knew how cross Daniel's parents got when he didn't do brilliantly at school.

Daniel's parents were professors. Both of them. His father was called Professor Trent and if only Daniel had been dead and buried in some interesting tomb somewhere, the Professor would have been delighted with him. He was an archaeologist who studied ancient tribes and in particular their burial customs and he was incredibly clever. But Daniel wasn't mummified or covered in clay so the Professor didn't have much time for him. Daniel's mother (who was also called Professor Trent) was a philosopher who had written no less than seven books on The Meaning of Meaning and she too was terribly clever and found it hard to understand that her son was just an ordinary boy who sometimes got his sums wrong and liked to play football.

The house they lived in was tall and grey and rather dismal, and looked out across the river to the university where both the professors worked, and to the zoo. As often as not when Daniel came home from school there was nobody there, just notes propped against the teapot telling him what to unfreeze for supper and not to forget to do his piano practice.

When you know you are a disappointment to your parents, your schoolfriends become very important. Fortunately Daniel had plenty of these. There was Joe whose father was a keeper in the Wellbridge

7

Zoo, and Henry whose mother worked as a chambermaid in the Queen's Hotel. And there was Sumi who was so gentle and so clever and never showed off even though she knew the answers to everything. And because it was Sumi who asked him, he went along to babysit at The Towers.

The Boothroyds' house was across the river in a wide, tree-lined street between the university and the zoo. They had been quite old when Basil was born and they dressed him like babies were dressed years ago. Basil slept in a barred cot with a muslin canopy and blue bows; his pillow was edged with lace and he had a silken quilt. And there he sat, in a long white nightdress, steaming away like a red and angry boil.

The Boothroyds left. Sumi and Daniel settled down on the sitting-room sofa. Sumi took out the list of spellings.

'Separate,' she said, and Daniel sighed. He was not very fond of separate.

But it didn't matter because at that moment Basil began to scream.

He screamed as though he was being stuck all over with red-hot skewers and by the time they got upstairs he had turned an unpleasant shade of puce and was banging his head against the side of the cot.

Sumi managed to gather him up. Daniel ran to warm his bottle under the tap. Sumi gave it to him and he bit off the teat. Daniel ran to fetch another. Basil took a few windy gulps, then swivelled round and knocked the bottle out of Sumi's hand.

It took a quarter of an hour to clean up the mess

8

and by the time they got downstairs again, Sumi had a long scratch across her cheek.

'Separate,' she said wearily, picking up the list.

'S . . . E . . . P . . .' began Daniel – and was wondering whether to try an A or an E when Basil began again.

This time he had been sick all over the pillow. Sumi fetched a clean pillow-case and Basil took a deep breath and filled his nappy. She managed to change him, kicking and struggling, and put on a fresh one. Basil waited till it was properly fastened, squinted – and filled it again.

It went on like this for the next hour. Sumi never lost her patience, but she was looking desperately tired and Daniel, who knew how early she got up each day to mind her little brothers and help tidy the shop before school, could gladly have murdered Basil Boothroyd.

At eight o'clock they gave up and left him. Basil went on screaming for a while and then – miracle of miracles – he fell silent. But when Daniel looked across at Sumi for another dose of spelling he saw that she was lying back against the sofa cushions. Her long dark hair streamed across her face and she was fast asleep.

Daniel should now have felt much better. Sumi was asleep, there was no need to spell separate and Basil was quiet. And for about ten minutes he did.

Then he began to worry. *Why* was Basil so quiet? Had he choked? Had he bitten his tongue out and bled to death?

Daniel waited a little longer. Then he crept upstairs and stood listening by the door.

Basil wasn't dead. He was snoring. Daniel was about to go downstairs again when something about the noise that Basil was making caught his attention. Basil was snoring, but he was snoring... nicely. Daniel couldn't think of any other way of putting it. It was a cosy, snuffling snore and it surprised Daniel because he didn't think that Basil could make any noise that wasn't horrid.

Daniel put his head round the door ... took a few steps into the room.

And stopped dead.

At first he simply didn't believe it. What had happened was so amazing, so absolutely wonderful, that it couldn't be real. Only it *was* real. Daniel blinked and rubbed his eyes and shook himself, but it was still there, curled up on the silken quilt: not a screaming, disagreeable baby, but the most enchanting bulldog puppy with a flat, wet nose, a furrowed forehead and a blob of a tail.

Daniel stood looking down at it, feeling quite light-headed with happiness, and the puppy opened its eyes. They were the colour of liquorice and brimming with soul. There are people who say that dogs don't smile, but people who say that are silly. The bulldog grinned. It sat up and wagged its tail. It licked Daniel's hands.

'Oh, I do so like you,' said Daniel to the little, wrinkled dog.

And the dog liked Daniel. He lay on his back so that Daniel could scratch his stomach; he jumped up to try and lick Daniel's face, but his legs were too short and he collapsed again. Daniel had longed and longed for a dog to keep him company in that tall, grey house to which his parents came back so late. Now it seemed like a miracle, finding this funny, loving, squashed-looking little dog in place of that horrible baby.

Because Basil had gone. There was no doubt about it. He wasn't in the cot and he wasn't under it. He wasn't anywhere. Daniel searched the bathroom, the other bedrooms... Nothing. Someone must have come in and taken Basil and put the little dog there instead. A kidnapper? Someone wanting to hold Basil to ransom? But why leave the little dog? The Boothroyds might not be very bright, but they could tell the difference between their baby and a dog.

I must go and tell Sumi, he thought, and it was only then that he became frightened, seeing what was to come. The screaming parents, the police, the accusations. Perhaps they'd be sent to prison for not looking after Basil properly. And where *was* Basil? He might be an awful baby, but nobody wanted him harmed.

Daniel tore himself away from the bulldog and studied the room.

How could the kidnappers have got in? The front door was locked, so was the back and the window was bolted. He walked over to the fireplace. It was the old-fashioned kind with a wide chimney. But that was ridiculous – even if the kidnappers had managed to come down it, how could they have got the baby off the roof?

Then he caught sight of something spilled in the empty grate: a yellowish coarse powder, like bread-crumbs.

He scooped some up, felt it between his fingers,

11

put it to his nose. Not breadcrumbs. Goldfish food. He knew because the only pet his parents had allowed him to keep was a goldfish he'd won in a fair, and it had died almost at once because of fungus on its fins. And he knew too where the goldfish food came from: the corner pet shop, two streets away from his house. The old man who kept it made it himself; it had red flecks in it and always smelled very odd.

Daniel stood there and his forehead was almost as wrinkled as the little dog's. For the pet shop had been sold a week ago to a queer-looking woman. Daniel had seen her moving about among the animals and talking to herself. She'd been quite alone, just the sort of woman who might snatch a baby to keep her company. He'd read about women like that taking babies from their prams while their mothers were inside a supermarket. The police usually caught them – they weren't so much evil as crazy.

Daniel gave the puppy a last pat and went downstairs. Sumi was still asleep, one hand trailing over the side of the sofa. For a moment he wondered whether to wake her. Then he let himself very quietly out of the house and began to run.

# Chapter Three

He ran across the bridge, turned into Park Avenue where his house was, then plunged into the maze of small streets that led between the river and the market place. Sumi's parents' shop was in one of these, and close by, on the corner, was the pet shop.

Daniel had been inside it often when the old man owned it, but now he stood in front of it, badly out of breath and very frightened. It was dusk, the street-lamps had just been lit and he could see the notice above the door.

UNDER NEW MANAGEMENT, it said. PROPRIETOR; MISS H. TENBURY-SMITH.

There was no one downstairs; the blinds were drawn, but upstairs, he could see one lighted window.

Daniel put his hand up to ring the bell and dropped it again. His knees shook, his heart was pounding. Suddenly it seemed to him that he was quite mad coming here. If the woman in the shop had taken Basil, she was certainly not going to hand him over to a schoolboy. She was much more likely to kidnap him too or even murder him so that he couldn't tell the police.

He was just turning away, ready to run for it, when the door suddenly opened and a woman stood in the hallway. She was tall with frizzy hair and looked brisk and eager like a hockey mistress in an old-fashioned girls' school. And she was smiling!

'Come in, come in,' said Miss Tenbury-Smith. 'I've been expecting you.'

Daniel stared at her. 'But how . . .' he stammered. 'I mean, I've come—'

'I know why you've come, dear boy. You've come to thank me. How people can say that children nowadays are not polite, I cannot understand. I expect you'd like some tea?'

Quite stunned by all this, Daniel followed her through the dark shop, with its rustlings and squeakings, and up a narrow flight of stairs. Miss Tenbury-Smith's flat was cosy. A gas fire hissed in the grate, there were pictures of middle-aged ladies in school blazers, and on the mantelpiece, a framed photograph with its face turned to the wall.

'Unless you'd rather have fruit juice?' she went on. And as Daniel continued to stare at her, 'You're admiring my dressing-gown. It's pure batskin – a thousand bats went into its making. And in case you're wondering – *every single one of those bats died in its sleep*. I would never, never wear the skin of an animal that had not passed away peacefully from old age. Never!'

But now Daniel felt he had to get to the point. 'Actually, it's about the Boothroyd baby that I've come,' he said urgently.

'Well, of course it is, dear boy. What else?' said Miss Tenbury-Smith. 'You're quite certain that tea would suit you?'

'Yes . . . tea would be fine. Only, please, Miss Tenbury-Smith, my friend is in such trouble. We're

14

babysitting and the Boothroyds are due back any minute and there'll be such a row, so could you possibly give Basil back? Just this once?'

'Give him back? Give him *back*?' Her voice had risen to an outraged squeak.

'Well, you swapped him . . . didn't you? You kidnapped him?' But Daniel's voice trailed away, suddenly uncertain.

Miss Tenbury-Smith put down the teapot. Her slightly protruding eyes had turned stony. Her eyebrows rose. 'I . . . *kidnapped* . . . Basil Boothroyd?' she repeated, stunned. Her long nose twitched and she looked very sad. 'I was so sure we were going to be friends, Daniel,' she said, and he looked up, amazed that she should know his name. 'And now this!' She sighed. 'Now listen carefully. When you have kidnapped somebody you have got him. You agree with that? He is with you. He is part of your life.'

'Yes.'

'And would you imagine that a person in their right mind would want to have Basil? Even for five minutes? Or are you suggesting that I am *not* in my right mind?'

'No . . . no . . . But—'

'I came to Wellbridge to Do Good, Daniel. It's my mission in life to make the world a better place.' She tapped the side of her long nose. 'It hurts, you know, to be misunderstood.'

'So you didn't swap Basil for the little dog?'

'Swapped him? Of course I didn't swap him. Oh, I had so *hoped* that you would be my friend. I'm really very fond of boys with thin faces and big eyes.

15

Some people would say your ears are on the large side, but personally I like large ears. But I can't be doing with a friend who is stupid.'

'I want to be your friend,' said Daniel, who did indeed want it very much. 'But I don't understand. You're . . . Are you . . .? Yes, of course; I see. You're a witch!'

Miss Tenbury-Smith began to pour out the tea, but she had forgotten the tea-bags.

'Well, I'm glad you see something,' she said. 'But the point is, I'm not just a witch; I'm a witch who means to make the world a better place. Now let me ask you a question. Have you ever seen a kangaroo throwing a bomb into a supermarket, killing little children?'

'No, I haven't.'

'Good. Have you ever seen an anteater hijack an aeroplane?'

'No.'

'Or a hamster go round knocking old ladies on the head and stealing their handbags? Have you ever seen a coshing hamster?'

'No.'

'Exactly. It's very simple. Animals are not wicked. It is people who are wicked. So you might think wicked people should be killed.'

'Yes . . . I suppose so.'

'However, killing is bad. It is wicked. And I'm not a wicked witch, I'm a good witch. And I do good by turning wicked people into animals.'

She leant back, pleased with herself, and took a sip of hot water.

16

Daniel stared at her. 'You mean . . . you changed Basil into a dog? Into that lovely dog?'

'Yes, I did. I'm so glad you liked it. I adore bulldogs; the way they snuffle and snort, and those deep chests. When you take a bulldog on a ship, you have to face them upwind because their noses are so flat. It's the only way they can breathe. Of course, when I changed that dreadful baby, I was just limbering up. Wellbridge is a little damp, being so low-lying, and I wasn't sure how it would affect my Knuckle of Power.' She stuck out her left hand and showed him a purple swelling on the joint. 'If you get rheumatism on your knuckle it can make things very tricky. But it all went like a dream. I really did it for that pretty friend of yours – so polite, and such a nice shop her parents keep with everything higgledy-piggledy, not like those boring supermarkets. Poor children, I thought, they're going to have such a horrible evening.'

'Yes, but you see it's going to be much more horrible if the Boothroyds come and find Basil gone. There'll be such trouble. So, please, could you change Basil back? If you can?'

'If I *can*?' said the witch, looking offended. 'Really, Daniel, you go too far. And actually I was going to change Basil back in any case, sooner or later, because babies aren't really wicked. To be wicked you have to know right from wrong and choose wrong, and babies can't do that. But I cannot believe that the Boothroyds wouldn't rather have the little dog for a night or two. He's completely house-trained, did you know?'

'Honestly, Miss Tenbury-Smith, I'm sure they wouldn't. I'm really sure.'

'Extraordinary,' said the witch, shaking her head to and fro. 'Well, in that case, let's see what we can do. Just wait while I change my clothes.'

# Chapter Four

'Well, you seem to be right,' said Heckie as they approached The Towers. 'The dear Boothroyds do not sound happy.'

All the lights were on and one could hear Mrs Boothroyd's screams halfway down the street.

'Oh, poor Sumi!'

'Now don't worry,' said the witch, who had changed into her school blazer and pleated skirt. 'I shall pretend to be a social worker. That always goes down well. Just follow me.'

Inside the Boothroyds' sitting-room, a fat policeman was writing things in a notebook and a thin policeman was talking to headquarters on his walkie-talkie. Mrs Boothroyd was yelling and hic-cupping and gulping by turns, and Mr Boothroyd was blustering and threatening to do awful things to Sumi's family. Sumi sat crouched on the sofa, her head in her hands. Between her shoes one could just see the dark, wet nose of the bewildered little dog.

'Now, my dear good people, what is all this about?' enquired Heckie briskly. 'I found this poor boy wandering about in the street quite beside himself.' She pointed to the letters WAW on her blazer. 'I am from the Wellbridge Association for Welfare,' she went on, 'and we cannot be doing with that kind of thing.'

'My baby's been kidnapped! My little treasure! My bobbikins!' screeched Mrs Boothroyd.

'And it's all these children's fault!' roared Mr Boothroyd.

'Nonsense,' said Heckie. 'He'll just have got mislaid somewhere. It often happens with babies.'

'We've searched high and low, Miss,' said the fat policeman.

But the little bulldog had heard Heckie's voice. He crawled out from under the sofa and as she crouched down to him, he leapt on to her lap.

'Who let that brute in again?' raged Mr Boothroyd – and Sumi blushed and turned her head away.

'Dogs give you fleas! They give you worms behind the eyeballs,' screeched Mrs Boothroyd.

Heckie looked hard at the Boothroyds. She was angry, but she was also amazed. In spite of what Daniel had said, she hadn't really believed that they would prefer Basil to the little dog. Then she gathered up the puppy and went to the door which Daniel was holding open for her, and out into the garden.

For an animal witch, turning nice animals into silly people is much harder than the other way round. Heckie's eyes were sad as she shook off her left shoe so that her Toe of Transformation could suck power from the earth. Then she spoke softly to the bulldog, waiting till his tail stopped wagging and his eyes were closed. Only when he slept did she touch him with her Knuckle of Power and say her spells.

Ten minutes later, Heckie returned to the drawing-room. She had held the puppy close to her chest, but she carried Basil at arm's length like a tray. His nightdress was covered in black streaks, he was bawling – but he was quite unharmed.

'My lambkin, my prettikins, my darling!' shrieked Mrs Boothroyd, covering him with squelchy kisses.

'My son, my boy!' slobbered Mr Boothroyd.

'Where was he, Miss?' asked the fat policeman.

'At the back of the coalshed,' said Heckie. 'The obvious place to look for a baby, I'd have thought.'

'But how did he get there?'

Heckie felt sorry for the fat policeman who so much wanted to have something to put in his notebook. 'You want to look for a tall man with red hair, blue eyes, a black moustache, an orange anorak and purple socks. I saw him climbing over the garden wall. It'll be him who put Basil among the coals.'

'But what would be the motive?' asked the policeman with the walkie-talkie.

'Oh, that's easy,' said Heckie. 'Revenge. Someone getting their own back. He'll have bought one of Mr Boothroyd's bath plugs and found it leaked. You know what it's like when all the hot water drains away and you're sitting in an empty tub all cold and blue with goosepimples . . .'

But when they had dropped Sumi off in the taxi Mr Boothroyd had been forced to pay for, Heckie turned to Daniel, looking thoughtful and serious.

'You know, Daniel, I shall have to change my plans entirely. I had no idea people would make such a fuss and be so unreasonable. I thought they'd come to me and say: "Please, Heckie, would you turn my drunken husband into a dear chimpanzee?" Or: "We feel that Uncle Phillip, who is a handbag snatcher, would do better as a Two-toed Sloth." That kind of

21

thing. But now I see it isn't so. I shall have to work in the *strictest* secrecy. Evil-doers will have to be *flushed out*!' She peered at Daniel. 'Might one ask why you are snivelling? Is it because there's no one at home?'

Sumi's parents had been there to welcome her, but Daniel's house, as the taxi drew up, was silent and dark.

Daniel shook his head. 'I don't mind being alone.' He wiped away the tear in the corner of his eye. 'It's that lovely bulldog. I miss him so *much*!'

Heckie examined his face in the light of the lamp. 'You know, you have the right ideas. Yes, I think I might be able to use you. For I have to tell you, Daniel, that I have just had a vision. I see a band of Wickedness Hunters! Children and witches together, uniting to rid Wellbridge of Wickedness! Yes, yes, I see it all. But first, dear boy, I must get myself a familiar. What a good thing that tomorrow is Sunday. Come after breakfast and we'll go to the zoo!'

# Chapter Five

When Daniel called at the shop the following morning, he found Heckie feeding her hat.

After the quarrel with Dora Mayberry, Heckie had crept back and gathered up her Ribbon Snakes and King Snakes and the Black Mamba, and they now lived in a tank in a room behind the shop, eating boiled eggs and hissing and not being a trouble to anyone. It would have been easy for her to weave them together again and wear them on her head, but she hadn't the heart, and because she knew that Daniel was a boy who could be trusted with people's sorrows, she told him what had happened and how dreadfully she missed her friend.

'We had such plans, Dora and I. She was going to have a little business making garden gnomes and nice things like that, and gradually fill the park with interesting statues. Only statues of wicked people, of course. Dora was Good, like me. Come and see her picture.'

She took Daniel up to the sitting-room and showed him the photo of Dora which she had turned with its face to the wall. The stone witch, with her square jaw and piggy eyes, was not beautiful, but Daniel said she looked interesting, like a prize fighter.

'Yes, indeed,' said Heckie, and sighed. 'And you should have seen her on the netball field! But it's all over between us.' And she turned the photo back to face the wall.

When they had fed the other animals in the shop, Heckie went to the larder to fetch a carrot. The carrot was about half a metre long and as thick as a thigh and scarcely fitted into the shopping basket, which was a tartan one on wheels, but Heckie said it would do for their lunch.

'My friend grows them for me. She's a garden witch – there's nothing she can't do with vegetables, but they do come out rather big.'

'What I was wondering,' said Daniel as they wheeled the carrot towards the zoo, 'was why you *need* a familiar? I mean, they're animals that help witches to do their magic, aren't they – and you changed Basil all right without one?'

'I don't *need* one, but I *want* one. And nothing ordinary like black cats or toads. I bet Dora's trailing round with a bontebok by now at the very least.'

Wellbridge Zoo was small, but pretty and well-kept, with flower-beds between the cages. Daniel went there often because his friend Joe, whose father was a keeper in the ape house, could get him in free.

'Now to business,' said Heckie when they had paid and gone through the turnstile. 'You know what we're looking for?'

'An animal that's fierce?'

'Well, not so much fierce as powerful. Mean. Strange and perhaps a little throbbing; that kind of thing.'

But the sea lions, lying about like old sofas, did not look very mean or throbbing and nor did the giraffes with their knock knees and film-star eyes.

24

They passed the aviary and though the cassowary looked interesting with its flabby black wattles and dirty feet, Heckie did not think she really wanted a bird.

'All that flapping is not very good for magic, I have found.'

But when they got to the hyena, pacing up and down in its cage, Heckie's face lit up. 'Now that is something! The way its back end just trails away and those sinister spots, and the *smell*!'

She wrote something in her notebook and they crossed over to the big enclosure which housed the kangaroos and wallabies – great, rat-coloured beasts with huge feet and mad, twitchy ears which Heckie liked enormously. 'Oh, I wish I was an Australian witch,' she cried. 'Everything over there is so queer and extinct-looking!'

The animal houses were closer together now and Heckie was running from cage to cage, as excited as a child in a toy shop. There were penguins jumping from rock to rock with their feet together like loopy waiters; there was a rusty numbat shovelling up ants – and there was a camel in front of which she stood for a long time. It was a bull camel, tall and sneery with lumpy knees and a lower lip full of froth. Bits of dirty straw stuck to its hump, and a low rumble like thunder came from its throat.

'I want this camel,' said Heckie. 'I want it terribly. But I'm going to be sensible. I'm going to be practical. I'm going to be *brave*.'

Daniel could see how hard it was for her to tear herself away from the camel, but in the reptile house she cheered up again. It was a silent, sinister place and every one of the animals looked as though it would help one to do magic: the crocodile, smiling in its sleep, the Bearded Basilisk, the iguana like a shrunken dinosaur . . .

In the ape house, they saw what seemed to be a very small ape in blue jeans forking fresh straw on to the floor. This turned out to be Daniel's school-friend Joe, helping his father clean out the cages.

Joe's mother had died when he was born and his father had reared Joe like he reared one of his orphaned apes, carrying him round in a blanket, feeding him on bottles of milk and bananas. Joe's hair was ginger like the orang-utans' and fell over his face; there was no tree he couldn't climb, and when anyone annoyed him, he stuck out his lower lip and glowered exactly like a gorilla.

Daniel introduced him to Heckie who was very interested to hear that his father was a keeper.

'Tell me,' she said, 'are there any empty cages in this zoo? Spare cages? In case someone was to send in some animals in a hurry? Unexpectedly?'

Joe gave her a sharp look from under his hair and said, yes, there were. 'They're over by the West Gate, behind the tea place.'

He went on staring at Heckie as she talked to the monkeys and the apes. Joe understood animals almost as well as his father and he knew that the way they came up to Heckie and laid their faces against the bars and tried to take her hand was quite out of the ordinary.

'Is she an animal trainer or something?' he asked Daniel, and Daniel said that perhaps in a way she was.

'We'll just have our picnic now and have a think,' said Heckie when they had been right round the zoo. 'Perhaps your nice friend will lend us a saw to cut up this interesting carrot. Or shall we just go across the road to The Copper Kettle?'

Daniel thought this was a good idea and soon they were sitting at a corner table, eating cucumber sandwiches and looking at Heckie's list.

'Of course, the baboons are unbeatable. Those red and blue behinds!' Her eyes glinted. 'But I like the orang-utans too: the way their hair hangs down from their armpits . . .' She bit into her sandwich. 'You notice I'm being brave about the camel?'

Daniel nodded and suggested the Bearded Basilisk. 'It might fit better into the flat?'

'Yes, but reptiles are dreadfully snooty. Cold-blooded, you know. Oh dear, this is so *difficult*.'

Heckie was very quiet as they wheeled the carrot back across the river and the tip of her nose had gone quite white from the strain of deciding. But in the street behind Daniel's house, she stopped and stared at a shop window. It was a Do It Yourself shop full of tools and screws and bits of shelving.

Suddenly she hit her forehead with her hand. 'What an idiot I am, Daniel. What a complete fool! Why *choose* a familiar? Why not *make* one?'

'Oh yes,' said Daniel, his eyes shining. 'A Do It Yourself familiar! The first one in the world!'

And, terribly excited, they hurried back to Heckie's shop. Once she had made up her mind, Heckie wasted no time.

'Do you know what I'm going to make?'

Daniel shook his head.

27

'A dragon. Yes, honestly. Why not go for the best? A pocket dragon. Well, a bit bigger than that. Sort of between a rolling pin and a turkey in size. About the weight of a Stilton cheese. Oh, I can see him. Slightly fiery round the nostrils, you know, with green scales and golden claws! Let's get the pattern book and have a look.'

She went to the bookcase and got out a book called *Ferocious Dragons and Loathly Worms* and began to turn over the pages. There were pictures of silvery dragons like the ones that ate princesses and were killed by St George, and gloomy, evil-looking dragons with poisonous claws and fiery tongues. But the nicest dragons were the Chinese ones. They had shaggy heads like Tibetan terriers with their hair in topknots and big, bulging eyes and wide mouths chock-full of teeth which gave them a smiling look. Daniel had seen dragons like that painted on kites and liked them very much.

'Can you make a dragon from nothing?' he asked when they had decided that a Chinese dragon was what they wanted.

Heckie looked shocked. 'No, no, dear boy. I'm only a witch, you know. I can change anything into anything else, but I can't make things from nothing. What we'll do is find an animal that isn't *happy* any more. An animal that's tired of life – and then I can change it. To mess about with an animal that was enjoying life would be *quite* wrong.'

They went downstairs to the shop to see if there was an animal there that was bored with living, but there wasn't. So they went to the park because Heckie thought she remembered seeing a duck that

28

was no longer glad to be alive and, sure enough, there it was, sitting in a clump of rushes by the pond. It was a white Aylesbury drake; its eyes were filmed, its feathers were limp. The other ducks were swimming and diving and gobbling up bread that the children threw, but not this duck. This duck had turned its face to the wall.

Heckie put out an arm. The duck did not have time even for one 'quack' before it found itself zipped into the tartan shopping basket on wheels and bundled off to the pet shop.

'Can I watch you?' begged Daniel when they had unpacked the animal and set it down on the kitchen floor. 'Can I watch you make a dragon, please?'

'No, dear boy, I'm afraid not. And you wouldn't like it, you know. It's not just my knuckle – a lot of power comes from my feet. Things happen down there that are not suitable for anybody young.' She looked down at her toes and sighed. 'If you come tomorrow after school, the dragon should be ready,' said Heckie, and Daniel had to be content with that.

In the staffroom at Wellbridge Junior School, the deputy head was in a temper. 'I've had another letter from those professors complaining about Daniel's work. They say they'll take him away and send him to a private school if he doesn't do better.'

Miss Jones, who was Daniel's class teacher, put down her cup with a clatter. 'I wish they'd leave him alone. There's nothing wrong with Daniel; he's a thoroughly nice boy and his work's perfectly all right. If they spent a bit more time at home with him instead of nagging about his marks, there'd be some point.'

The deputy head nodded. 'I've gone past that house again and again and there's no one in. He's got a lost look in his eyes sometimes, that child. It's a pretty turn of affairs when the most deprived child in the class is the son of two rich professors.'

But when Miss Jones went to take her class for English, she thought that Daniel looked more cheerful than he had done of late – and indeed Daniel wasn't worrying about how he was going to do in the spelling test or whether he had passed his music exam. He was thinking that in a few hours he would see a dragon made out of an Aylesbury duck, and nobody who thinks that can look unhappy.

Of course, it would happen that on the one day on which Daniel was longing to get away, his parents were both in for tea.

'Well, how did you get on with your spelling test?' asked the Professor Trent who was Daniel's father. He was tall, with greying hair and a big nose.

'I hope you got ten out of ten,' said the Professor Trent who was Daniel's mother. She too was tall, with thick spectacles and a strong chin. When they were both standing looking down at him, Daniel felt a bit like a puppy who has made a puddle on the carpet.

'I got eight out of ten,' said Daniel, hoping that this would be all right, but it wasn't.

'Really?' said Daniel's father. 'And what words did you get wrong?'

Daniel sighed. 'Separate,' he said. 'And mystify.'

Daniel's parents thought this was odd. Daniel's

father had been able to spell mystify when he was four years old, and Daniel's mother said that surely when one understood that separate came from the Latin word *separare* there could be no difficulty. 'How many did Sumi get right?' she wanted to know.

'She got them all right. She always does.'

Both professors shook their heads. 'It seems extraordinary, Daniel, that a girl who does not even speak English at home should do so much better than you.'

Daniel said nothing. One day he meant to do something that would surprise his parents and make them proud of him – only what? If the house burnt down he could drag them from the flames (though they were rather large) and if there was a flood he could commandeer a boat and row them to safety. But so far there had been no fire, nor had the streets of Wellbridge turned into rivers, and sometimes Daniel thought that he would never be the kind of boy they wanted.

But when tea was over at last and he slipped out of the house, his face soon lost its pinched, dejected look. He took a deep breath of air and then he began to run.

Heckie seemed pleased to see him, but there was something a little odd in her manner.

'Is he finished? Have you done it?' asked Daniel eagerly.

'Of course,' said Heckie stiffly. 'What I do, I do. It's just . . .'

She led him upstairs and pointed to a dog basket she had brought up from the shop. The new familiar was sitting in it: a Chinese dragon about the size of a dachshund, with a black topknot of hair, big red eyes, fiery-looking nostrils and a pair of wings set close behind his ears.

'Oh!' said Daniel. 'He's beautiful! He's the most beautiful dragon in the world!'

'Yes, he is, isn't he,' said Heckie. 'Most of him, anyway . . .'

Daniel moved closer. The dragon's neck and shoulders were covered in green and golden scales, his pearl-tipped talons gripped the rim of the basket and his teeth were pointed and razor-sharp.

So far so good. It was the back of the dragon that was . . . unexpected.

Heckie cleared her throat. 'You see, I was just in the middle of changing him when the bell rang and it was the postman. You know how exciting it is when the postman rings. It might mean anything.' And Heckie blushed, for she had thought it might mean a letter from her friend Dora to say that she was sorry. 'I left the window open and the pages blew over in the book and . . . well, you see.'

'Yes,' said Daniel.

The front end of Heckie's new familiar was a dragon, but the back end was a worm. It was not an earthworm, it was a Loathly Worm like in the book – but it was a worm. There were twelve segments, each bulgy and carrying a pair of blobby legs, and though the dragon part was green and gold and scaly, the worm part was smooth and pale with faint pink spots.

'What shall I do?' asked Heckie, and Daniel was very touched that she, a witch of such power, should turn to him.

Daniel was usually a shy, uncertain boy, but he

32

knew exactly what she should do. 'Nothing! Please don't do anything. He's absolutely splendid as he is. I mean, any old witch could have a dragon for a familiar, but there can't be a single witch in the whole wide world who has a *dragworm*!'

Heckie smiled. 'I'm glad you feel like that, dear boy. Because, to tell the truth, it would hurt me now to change him. We'll soon get him trained up. He doesn't talk yet, but he understands quite a lot already.' She patted the dragworm's head and he shot out his forked tongue and licked her hand. 'We're in business, Daniel. You'll see. This time next year there won't be a single wicked person left in the length and breadth of Wellbridge!'

# Chapter Six

The Wellbridge Wickedness Hunters met in Heckie's sitting-room the following week.

Heckie had asked all the wizards and witches in the town to join and she had hoped that they might turn out to be a bit like Robin Hood and his Merry Men, but they had not. Mr Gurgle, a wizard who kept a grocer's shop in Market Square, was not at *all* like Robin Hood. He was a small, bald man who spent his time trying to make a cheese that could walk by itself. Not a cheese that could crawl – quite a lot of cheeses can do that – but a cheese that could walk right across a room without help. And Boris Chomsky, the mechanical wizard who serviced the hot air balloons the witches used, wasn't like Robin Hood either. He was a Russian with a long, sad face and wore a woollen muffler which was stained with oil because he worked in a garage.

Next to Boris sat Frieda Fennel, the garden witch who had grown Heckie's carrot. Frieda had green fingers which meant that anything would grow for her, but it was difficult to *stop* it growing. When Frieda scratched her ear or rubbed her neck, little buds or leafy shoots burst out where she had touched herself, so anyone sitting near her had to keep her tidy with garden shears.

And there was Madame Rosalia, who had been

Miss Witch 1965 and didn't let anyone forget it. Like most beauty queens, she was a show-off and was sitting with her chair floating halfway to the ceiling, just to be different. She kept a beauty parlour and always knew exactly what every witch should wear.

'Whiskers are in this year,' she would say, 'and moles are out,' which annoyed Heckie. If you wanted whiskers you wanted whiskers and if you wanted moles you wanted moles. What was in or out had nothing to do with it.

But if the witches and wizards were not quite what Heckie had hoped for, she felt cheered as soon as she looked at the sofa where the three children were sitting very straight with their knees together and their eyes bright as they took in what was going on.

Heckie had known at once that Sumi and Joe could be trusted, and when Daniel, during break at school, had told them who Heckie was, neither of them had been surprised.

'I knew,' said Joe. 'The way that gorilla tried to hold her hand.'

Sumi too had guessed. As she said, if someone has red hair they're not going to have a black moustache – Heckie had to have made up the man in the Boothroyds' garden. But though Joe was excited at once about becoming a Wickedness Hunter and tracking down evil people for Heckie to change, Sumi was not so sure.

'I don't know . . . People have souls, don't they?' she'd said, winding her long hair round her fingers. 'What happens to them when they're turned into animals?'

35

'Animals have souls too,' said Daniel. 'That bulldog puppy was bursting with soul.'

But Sumi was still troubled. 'I think it could go wrong. I think it could all go horribly wrong.'

But in the end, she'd agreed to join the club, if only to make herself useful. And already she had been useful. The mugs of tea that the witches and wizards were drinking all had tea-bags in them, and the biscuits they were eating came from her parents' shop.

And between the wizards and the children, sat the dragworm in his basket.

Heckie now made a speech. She welcomed everybody and said how pleased she was to see them, and then she told them the kind of person she was looking for.

'What I'm after,' she said, 'isn't someone who's just lost his temper and battered his bank manager to death with a hammer. Battering your bank manager to death with a hammer is not good, of course, but anyone can lose their temper and some bank managers are very annoying. What we're looking for is people who do evil day after day, knowing that they are doing it, and still going on.'

'Like flushers,' interrupted the cheese wizard, getting excited. 'Flushers want changing.'

'What's a flusher?' asked Joe – and Heckie explained that it was a person who flushed unwanted pets down the lavatory. 'Goldfish, newts – even terrapins. What's more, flushers often turn into dumpers,' she said, her eyes flashing. 'People who dump dogs on the motorway when they stop being dear little puppies. And dumpers we definitely want!'

She then became practical. 'You must remember that as soon as a wicked person becomes an animal, he has to be protected and cared for. If I turn an armed robber into a wombat he is not a wicked wombat, he is a *wombat* and has to be taken quickly to the zoo. And I shall need help for that.'

She looked at Chomsky, the mechanical wizard, who nodded and said he had a van which would do.

Madame Rosalia, whose underclothes were showing as she floated in her chair, now said that Heckie was wasting her time. 'Whatever you do there's always more and more wickedness in the world. Look at the newspapers! Every day there's some grandfather starving a child to death in an attic, or a hit and run motorist leaving a boy in the road. There's always been evil in the world and there always will be.'

For a moment, Heckie looked tired and sad. Witches only live for three hundred years and she knew better than anyone how much there was to do. Then she brightened. 'I think you forget,' she said, 'that I don't just have all you dear people to help me. I have my familiar!' She pointed to the drag-worm, still sitting peacefully in his basket. 'With a familiar like that, how can I fail?'

There was a pause. Then from up in the air, there came a titter.

'Come, come, Heckie, you don't think that funny-looking thing is going to be any use?'

'It would certainly be most unwise to expect anything from . . . er . . . *that*,' said the cheese wizard pompously.

'Poor thing, he'd be better dug in for manure,' said the garden witch.

It was exactly at this moment that there was a loud ring at the doorbell of the shop.

'Drat!' said Heckie. 'I put up a notice saying SHOP CLOSED. Why don't they go away?'

But whoever it was didn't go away. There was another loud peal of the bell.

'It's someone with a white Rolls-Royce,' said Joe, who had gone to the window. 'An absolute whopper, and there's a chauffeur driving it.'

Leaning out, the children could see the woman who was ringing the bell so impatiently. She was wearing a fur coat, white like her car, and her hair was piled up into a kind of tower and looked as though it had been sprayed with gold paint.

The bell rang for the third time.

'Oh, blast the woman! I'd better go and see.' Heckie opened the door and the dragworm decided to follow her. This was not so simple. His front end bounded out of the basket quickly enough, helped by the whirring of his little wings. But then he stopped and a frown appeared between his shaggy eyebrows. The worm part of him had twenty-four legs, a pair on each of his bulges, and it was not easy for him to decide which one to start walking with.

The wizards and witches tittered, and the children glared at them.

Then all at once, the legs on the third bulge from the end started to move, which set off all the others, and, suddenly looking very happy, the dragworm bounded and slithered down the stairs.

In the shop, Heckie tucked him up behind one of the food-bins so that no one could see him. Then she opened the door and the woman in the white fur coat swept in. She was carrying a birdcage with a cover which she took off. Inside was a large green and orange parrot.

'Where's Sam?' said the parrot, his head on one side.

'I want you to buy this bird,' said the woman in a bossy voice.

'I'm afraid I don't buy birds from private people. One can never be sure that they are not diseased.'

'This parrot is not diseased,' said the woman huffily, and once again the parrot said: 'Where's Sam?'

'Where *is* Sam?' asked Heckie.

'Sam was his owner. He's gone away and because I am a kind and caring person, I offered to find a home for the parrot. I'll take fifty pounds.'

Heckie was about to say no, but the parrot edged closer on his perch and she saw his eyes. 'I'll give you forty,' she said.

To her surprise, the woman took it and left.

'I'll see you later,' said Heckie to the parrot, and went back to the meeting.

'Now,' she said, when she was back in the sitting-room. 'Is there anything else—'

She broke off. Daniel and Sumi had both leapt to their feet and run towards the door.

'Oh, what has *happened*?' cried Daniel.

The dragworm had managed to get back upstairs but there was something terribly wrong with him. His breath came in rasping gasps, his wings were limp and the hair on his topknot had turned quite white! Worst of all was his wormy end. It had been smooth and pale with gentle pink splodges. Now all the splodges were horribly inflamed, raised up from the skin like boils, and the centre of every one was full of pus.

Up to now, Heckie's familiar had never made a sound, but as they carried him back to his basket, his head fell back and from his poor, sick throat there came a tragic and despairing: '*Quack!*'

Nobody laughed. Even the witches and wizards who had jeered knew that when people are in trouble they often go back to their childhood, crying or calling for their mothers. The dragworm had gone back to *his* early life – the life when he was a duck.

Heckie was beside herself, running backwards and forwards with medicines and blankets, and it was the garden witch who said: 'Wait! I've seen this before. Seen it with Mad Millicent's familiar.' She scratched her head, but Heckie was far too worried to clip off the green shoot that burst out between her eyebrows. 'The fiercest witch in the east, she was, and her familiar with her.'

The cheese wizard nodded. 'That's right. He was a lizard and he'd come on just like that when there was some evil in the place. And Wall-eyed William's familiar too. An eagle, he was – a real brute and he used to come out in great red boils under his feathers. A proper help it was to William.'

'You mean . . .' Heckie looked up and she was blushing. 'Are you saying . . .? Oh, surely not. I'm only an ordinary witch. Surely I couldn't have made one of . . . you know . . . *them?*'

40

The wizards and witches nodded and looked at Heckie with a new respect.

'Made what?' Joe wanted to know.

'A detector! A wickedness detector! A familiar who comes over queer when he meets anyone wicked!' cried Heckie, clapping her hands, and Daniel felt quite cross. How could she look so pleased when the dragworm was suffering? Though actually he was beginning to look a little better: some of the black was returning to his hair and the spots were fading. 'A wickedness detector. Oh my, oh my! So we'll always know for certain whether somebody's evil or not! Well, there's nothing to stop us now!'

'Yes, but who *made* him come out in spots like that?' asked Joe.

Everybody looked at everybody else. In the silence, they could hear the parrot still asking: 'Where's Sam? Where's Sam?'

'Of course!' cried Heckie. 'The woman in the shop. The woman with the white Rolls-Royce. After her, children! Find out everything you can about her. Everything!'

# Chapter Seven

It didn't take the children long to trace the owner of the white Rolls-Royce. Her name was Mrs Winneypeg and she was one of the richest women in Wellbridge. She didn't just have a white Rolls-Royce, she had a white BMW and a white Jaguar. She lived alone in a house with seven bedrooms and a private swimming pool and owned seven fur coats, three of them mink.

And she made her money looking after old people.

'But that's a good thing to do, surely?' said Daniel when they had reported back to Heckie. 'So why was the dragworm so ill when he saw her?'

Could the dragworm be wrong? Nobody thought so, but it was odd all the same.

'We'll just go on sniffing round,' said Heckie. 'For one thing, I'd like to know why she sold that parrot.'

For the parrot still said nothing except: 'Where's Sam?' and had to be coaxed to eat.

The way Mrs Winneypeg looked after old people was to run a number of rest homes where they could go when they were too old or ill to look after themselves. They were called the Sundown Homes and it so happened that one of them was at the bottom of Daniel's street. It was made up of three old houses knocked together and from the front it looked nice enough. The brass plate was brightly polished, the paintwork looked new.

But now Daniel slipped in to the alleyway behind the houses, where no one ever went, and here it was very different. The windows were dirty, the dustbins were overflowing, and one could see the wispy grey heads of the old people herded together in a dingy room.

The children began to ask questions in the neighbouring shops and to hang round the home to see if they could find out more, but it seemed that nobody wanted to talk about Mrs Winneypeg and her Sundown Homes. And then, on the third day, when Daniel just 'happened' to be loitering there after school, the door burst open and a nurse in a blue uniform came stumbling down the steps and bumped right into Daniel. She was Irish and very young, and she was crying.

'That place – that awful place!' she sobbed. 'I can't stand it any more. I'm leaving.'

And because Daniel had a listening sort of face and she had to talk to someone, she told him what it was like in the building she'd just left. She told him about the bullying and the disgusting food and the way the old people were sent up to bed at six o'clock to save the heating. She told him about Miss Merrick who so loved flowers and had been told she could have a window-box, and then when she spilled a little bit of earth because her hands were shaky, Mrs Winneypeg had screamed at her and taken the window-box away. She told him about Major Holden who'd fought in two world wars and asked for some boot polish because he liked to keep himself

43

neat even if he couldn't see too well, and who'd been locked in his room for making a fuss.

'She's a fiend, that Mrs Winneypeg – she ought to burn in hell,' said the nurse, mopping her eyes. 'All her homes are like that and the poor old things never get out once she's got hold of them. She takes their pension books and their savings and burns the letters they write, so no one ever knows.'

'Can't the council do anything?' Daniel asked.

The nurse shrugged. 'People have complained, but she's buttered up the councillors for years. I meant to stick it out, but that old chap and his parrot was the last straw. Such a nice bloke – been in the navy all his life and no bother to anyone. He only came because she said he could keep his parrot, and now she's told him it's dead. You should see him – he won't last a month the way he's going. And the parrot isn't dead! I saw the chauffeur put it in the boot of her car. She'll have flogged it or torn its feathers out for a hat.'

'Is his name Sam?' asked Daniel. 'The gentleman with the parrot?'

The nurse blew her nose and looked at Daniel. 'Yes,' she said. 'It is.'

So now they knew why the dragworm had come out in those dreadful boils. Mrs Winneypeg was what is called a Granny Farmer, and there is probably nothing more unpleasant in the world.

But Mrs Winneypeg was about to get a big surprise.

\*

44

A week later, a new resident arrived at the Wellbridge Sundown Home. Miss Smith was ancient and tottery and deaf – and she was very rich. Mrs Winneypeg was waiting to greet her and her greedy eyes lit up when she saw the poor old thing helped out of the taxi by her great-nephew. *She* wasn't going to give any trouble, that was certain! And the nephew and his family were off to Australia, she'd said on the phone, so there'd be no relatives to poke and pry.

'It's very kind of you to let me stay in your lovely home,' quavered Miss Smith – and winked at Daniel. Madame Rosalia might be a show-off, but there was nothing she couldn't do with make-up. Heckie's wrinkles would have fooled anyone; her hair was white; brown blotches covered her skin.

'Not at all. I'm sure you'll be very happy with us,' said Mrs Winneypeg in a plummy voice. 'You've brought some money with you? Cash, I like – it makes less work.'

Miss Smith fumbled in her handbag.

'That'll be fine,' said Mrs Winneypeg, grabbing some notes. 'Now if your dear nephew will just say goodbye, we'll soon make you comfortable.'

An hour later, Heckie was in a small bedroom in which four beds had been shoved so close together that you could hardly move between them. Three wispy-haired ladies in nightdresses sat one on each bed, shivering with cold.

'You shouldn't have come,' said one of them hopelessly. 'It's a dreadful place this.'

'Oh, I expect we can soon get things cheered up,' said Heckie. But she was so angry she could hardly speak. She'd decided not to do anything till she was sure that the home was as bad as the young nurse said. Now she knew that it was worse. She'd seen Major Holden tied to his chair because he liked to wander about and the staff said he got in the way. She'd seen old Sam force-fed with revolting stew because he wouldn't eat since he lost his parrot and Mrs Winneypeg didn't want him to die and bring the doctor to ask awkward questions. She'd seen a woman as thin as a skeleton slip on the bathroom floor and be scolded for carelessness . . .

At eight, a nurse came to turn out the light.

'I'd like a hot-water bottle,' said Heckie. 'I'm cold.'

'A *hot-water bottle*!' said the nurse. 'You must be out of your mind!'

All the kind nurses had left; only the cruel ones could stand working for Mrs Winneypeg and most of them weren't real nurses at all.

At midnight, Heckie got up and stood by the window. Everything was ready; all her helpers knew what to do. Daniel and Sumi were taking it in turns to mind the shop and sit with the dragworm; Joe had 'borrowed' his father's keys to the West Gate of the zoo and would come with Boris in his van to drive whatever it was to safety.

Only what *was* it going to be? Heckie wasn't sure. Nothing *cuddly*, of course. 'I'll just have to see how I feel when the time comes,' she said, and went back to bed.

Breakfast was lumpy porridge and dry bread.

'I want some butter,' said Heckie. 'I've paid good money to be here and I want some butter on my bread.'

46

After breakfast she said she'd like to go out for a little walk and at eleven she wanted a nice cup of coffee.

By lunchtime it was clear that something would have to be done about Miss Smith and the matron went to ring Mrs Winneypeg.

'She's a troublemaker, Mrs Winneypeg. I don't know what to do with her.'

'Do with her? Do what we always do,' snapped Mrs Winneypeg. 'Undress her, take her teeth out and shut her in her room.'

'Well, I tried . . .' Matron broke off, not really able to explain why it wasn't easy to undress Miss Smith. 'Her teeth don't *take* out,' she complained.

'All right; I'm coming anyway at three o'clock to do the accounts. I'll soon sort her out.'

And Heckie, who had been listening at the door, held up three fingers to Boris, waiting in the street in his parked van, and settled down to wait.

The residents were sitting in a circle in the lounge when the white Rolls-Royce drew up in front of the door. Heckie could see the way they cowered at the sight of it and her chin went up.

'Listen,' she said quickly. 'How many of you can stand up without help? How many of you can walk?'

The circle of faces stared at her blankly.

'Come on,' she said. 'Some of you can, I know. I've seen you.'

Still the poor browbeaten creatures just stared at her. Then slowly, Major Holden's hand went up; then Sam's . . . then those of the ladies who shared Heckie's room – until almost everybody's hand was raised.

47

'Good,' said Heckie. 'Because I'm going to have a few words with Mrs Winneypeg and I want you to stand quite close in a circle. I need her to come right up to me – I don't want her running away. And I don't want . . . anything else running away either. Can you do that?'

The old people nodded. A little colour had come into their faces and Major Holden put up his hand in a salute.

The door opened and Mrs Winneypeg came into the room. She saw all the residents dozing as usual, and she marched straight up to Miss Smith.

'Now then, I hear you've been making trouble,' she said. 'Just exactly what is the matter?'

Heckie rose from her chair. 'Everything is the matter! Just exactly everything. This place is a disgrace. The food is revolting, the staff are unkind and you are a vicious woman!'

Mrs Winneypeg's mouth opened; her chins quivered. 'How dare you! How *dare* you speak to me like that!' She marched towards Heckie which was exactly what Heckie wanted. And the old people had heard and understood. They were doing what Heckie had asked. One by one, with their walking frames and their sticks, they stood in a circle round Heckie and Mrs Winneypeg. They were frail and tottery, but there were a lot of them.

'Well, I do dare. Why can't Major Holden have some boot polish when he's paid you thousands of pounds? Why did you take away Miss Merrick's window-box? And where is Mr Sam's parrot, answer me that?'

'Why you . . . you disgusting old woman. I'll have

48

you put away! I'll have you put in a loony bin. I'll ring the hospital and tell them to come with a strait-jacket.'

This threat had always worked before, but Miss Smith only laughed. 'Try it! Just you try it!'

Mrs Winneypeg blinked because Miss Smith seemed taller somehow and her voice had changed. But she moved forward and grabbed Heckie's arm.

And now Heckie had her. Her own free arm came round Mrs Winneypeg's fat throat. She kicked off her slipper and her toe curled and throbbed with the power that came from it. Mrs Winneypeg was scared now, she wanted to get away, but she was caught in a ring of old people. If she pushed through, someone would probably keel over and die and that meant doctors and people asking questions. And Heckie's grip was tightening. Her knuckle glowed like a ring of flame!

'Sploosh!' spluttered Mrs Winneypeg. 'Shluroop . . . *Oink!*'

And then it was over! At the last minute, Heckie had known exactly what would turn out best. And as they saw what had happened, there appeared on the faces of the old people a look of wonder, and one by one, their wrinkled faces broke into smiles.

But of course no one believed them afterwards. When Mrs Winneypeg had been gone a few days and the police came, and the inspectors from the council, no one believed a bunch of old people when they explained what had happened. Old people have fancies, everyone knows that. But the inspectors were so shocked by what they found in the Sundown Homes that they closed them then and there and moved the residents to council homes where they were properly cared for and had plenty to do. Miss Merrick was given a little bit of garden and Major Holden was put in charge of all the shoe cleaning, not just his own, so that everybody looked smart. And Sam's parrot stopped saying: 'Where's Sam?' and said some other things instead – things it is better not to mention because he'd been at sea with Sam for many years and had picked up some very fruity oaths.

But still no one believed the old ladies and the old gentlemen. Not even when a brand new warthog turned up in the Wellbridge Zoo – a warthog with a greedy snout and blue eyes and a way of banging its back parts furiously against the sides of the cage. Not even then.

# Chapter Eight

A new statue had appeared in Kidchester Town Park.
It was made of marble and very lifelike. You could
almost feel the hair on its moustache and the waxy
blobs inside its ears.

The council thought that the statue had been put
up by the Lord Mayor and the Lord Mayor thought
it had been put up by some ladies who called themselves the Friends of Kidchester and wanted to make
their town a beautiful place.

But the statue hadn't been put up by any of these
people. It had been dragged there in the middle of
the night by the stone witch, Dora Mayberry, who
had been Heckie's friend.

Dora had found a nice garden gnome business
in Kidchester which was about thirty miles from
Wellbridge. She made dwarves and fairies and mermaids for people to put round their garden ponds,
and in her spare time she tried to Do Good because
that was what she and Heckie said that they would
do. When she turned Henry Hartington to marble
and put him in the park, she was certainly making
the world a better place. She had heard Henry's wife
scream night after night while he beat her, and seen
his children run out of their house with awful
bruises, and when she met him rolling home from

the pub, she had simply looked at him in a certain way and that was that.

But she was lonely. She missed Heckie all the time. Dora was shy – she was apt to grunt rather than speak and this made it difficult to make new friends. Far from having a bontebok for a familiar, Dora didn't have a familiar at all. What she did have was a ghost: a miserable, wispy thing which had come with the old wardrobe Dora had bought to hang her clothes in. The ghost was a tree spirit who had stayed in her tree when the woodmen came with their axes, and floated about between the coathangers, begging Dora not to chop down the wardrobe.

'I wonder if I should write to Heckie,' said Dora to herself as she lowered a soya sausage into boiling water for her supper. 'But why doesn't *she* write to me?'

Then she went out to the shed to feed her hat. She too had gathered up the snakes that hissed and slithered on the lawn after the quarrel and brought them with her to her new home. But the hat was really the only pet that Dora had so she was feeding it too much and it was getting fat. The Black Mamba was like a barrel – soon it would be impossible to tie it into a bow.

Oh dear, thought Dora, nothing seems to be going right.

There was plenty to do in Kidchester. She had plans for Dr Franklin who kept twelve dogs in the basement of his laboratory and was doing the most horrible experiments with them. Not experiments to test new medicines, just experiments to test face creams for silly women who were afraid of getting old. Dr Franklin would look nice in granite and she knew exactly where she was going to put him: by the fountain in the shopping centre so that the children could climb on him and the pigeons would have somewhere to sit.

But nothing is much fun if you are lonely, not even Doing Good – and when poor Dora got back to the kitchen, the saucepan had boiled dry and the sausage had exploded in a most unpleasant way.

Should I move to Wellbridge in secret? thought Dora, scraping the sausage into the dustbin. Perhaps if we met by accident, Heckie and I would fall into each other's arms? But if she cut me dead, I couldn't bear it.

And poor Dora stood rubbing her nose, not knowing what to do.

# Chapter Nine

Warthogs are not beautiful, with their hairy grey bodies and messy snouts, but the new warthog which had arrived in Wellbridge Zoo was very popular. Lots of people came and watched it snort and snuffle and wallow in its trough, and the way it ignored the other warthog in the cage, barging into him as though he wasn't there, made everybody laugh. Perhaps it was the mysterious way the animal had arrived, sent by an unknown person as a gift to the zoo, that made people so interested. It had turned up in the middle of the night with a label round its neck which said MY NAME IS WINNIE. But whatever the reason, it certainly pulled in the crowds.

The dragworm, meanwhile, settled down happily in Heckie's shop. Everyone made a fuss of him, even the wizards and witches who had sneered, but he was not at all conceited. What he liked best was a quiet life, sleeping in his basket, going for careful walks with enough time to think about which of his legs was which – and having baths. Because of having been a duck, the dragworm loved to be in the water, and he was never happier than when he was sitting in Heckie's bathtub with Sumi washing his hair and Daniel scrubbing his back.

Heckie was still hoping that he would learn to

talk. Familiars often do and it is a great comfort to witches having someone to speak to when they are alone. But though he understood so much of what was said to him, the dragworm didn't open his mouth except to smile or yawn . . . or eat.

The dragworm was very fond of eating and what he ate (because he was, after all, a dragon) were princesses. Not real ones, of course; they would have been too big and anyway there weren't any in Wellbridge, but princesses made out of gingerbread which the children baked for him in Heckie's oven.

And it was a batch of these princesses which led Heckie to a man called Ralph Ticker who must have been about the nastiest person in the world.

Heckie wasn't after Ralph Ticker, she didn't even know he existed; she was after a mugger who had broken the skull of an old lady in a back lane and snatched her handbag. Heckie had decided to turn him into an okapi which is a beautiful animal halfway between a zebra and a giraffe. Wellbridge Zoo didn't have one, and she thought it would be nice if they did, so she spent the evenings tottering through the back alleyways of Wellbridge with a handbag full of money, waiting for the mugger to come, but so far he hadn't.

It was half-term. This was usually a bad time for Daniel. Sumi's aunts and uncles came to visit and she went on outings with her cousins, and Joe spent his time with his father in the zoo. Up to now, Daniel had dreaded the holidays which meant being alone in the tall, gloomy house while his parents went on going to the university.

But now it was Daniel who was the lucky one

because he could spend all his time in Heckie's shop. And it was Daniel who went to the market to buy half a dozen eggs, and Daniel who baked the princesses for the dragworm's supper.

He was whistling as he took the baking tray out of the oven and put in the currants for the princesses's eyes and the slithers of glacé cherries for their mouths. They had come out beautifully, with their crowns scarcely wonky at all, and as soon as they were cool enough, he scooped one out and put it on the dragworm's plate.

The dragworm bounded out of his basket; he put his snout down on the plate. Then he lifted his head and gave Daniel a look. And what the look said was: 'What exactly *is* this rubbish?'

Daniel was annoyed. 'They're absolutely fresh. I baked them myself. Now please eat up and don't make a fuss.'

He held the princess up to the dragworm's nose. The dragworm closed his eyes and shuddered. Then he turned his back on Daniel and climbed back into his basket.

It was at this moment that Heckie came back. She was not in a good temper because as she had been hovering in a dark lane, hoping for the mugger, a kind policeman had come and insisted on seeing her home.

'The dragworm's off his food. He won't eat his princess.' Daniel was upset. When your parents have told you for years and years that you're no good, you don't have much confidence, and Daniel was beginning to wonder if he'd done something wrong.

Heckie frowned. 'It doesn't look to me as if he's

sickening for anything. I hope he's not going to turn faddy.'

She broke off a leg and held it under the drag-worm's nose. Once again, the dragworm turned away and if he'd been able to speak, there's no doubt that what he would have said was: 'Yuk!'

Daniel now took Heckie into the kitchen and showed her exactly what he had used to bake the gingerbread: the flour, the sugar, the spices, the honey . . .

'And one of these,' he said, holding up the carton which had the words FRESH FARM EGGS stamped on the box. 'But it wasn't rotten. I smelled it carefully.'

There were five eggs left in the carton. Heckie picked up one and carried it to the window. 'Oh dear,' she said. 'Oh dear, oh *dear*!' And then: 'No wonder the poor dear creature wouldn't eat. For a wickedness detector an egg like this would be quite impossible to swallow.'

Daniel was puzzled. 'But surely . . . an egg can't be wicked, can it?'

Heckie was still holding the egg to the light and shaking her head to and fro. 'Not wicked, perhaps. But unhappy . . . full of bad vibes.'

'An *egg*!'

'Why not? An egg is made up of the same things as a person. Everything in nature can suffer – plants . . . seaweed . . . Seaweed can be absolutely *wretched*, you must have seen that.'

So they gave the dragworm some dog biscuits, which he ate, and it was decided that Daniel would go to the market first thing in the morning and ask the stallholder where she got her eggs.

'Because an unhappy egg means an unhappy chicken,' said Heckie, 'and an unhappy chicken we cannot and will not allow.'

The lady who had sold Daniel the fresh farm eggs was helpful. They came, she said, from the Tritlington Poultry Unit, about ten miles north of Wellbridge.

'They weren't bad, I hope?' she said anxiously. 'I've been promised they're not more than two days old.'

Daniel said, no, they weren't bad, not like that.

Two hours later, he got off the local train at Tritlington. It was eleven o'clock in the morning and the little station was almost empty. He asked the way to the poultry unit and was directed down a footpath which ran across two fields, and over the river, to some low, corrugated iron buildings.

'But he won't thank you for going there,' the station-master told Daniel.

'Who won't?' asked Daniel.

'Mr Ticker. The owner. Keeps himself to himself, does Mr Ticker.'

As Daniel made his way down the path, he wondered if he had been wise to come alone. But both Sumi and Joe were helping out at home, and anyway what was the use of being a Wickedness Hunter if you didn't *do* anything?

Mr Ticker's poultry unit was surprisingly large. There were two buildings, each of which looked more like an aircraft hangar or a railway shed than a farm. A high fence surrounded the area and there were notices saying: KEEP OUT and TRESPASSERS WILL BE PROSECUTED. Daniel's heart was beating rather fast, but he told himself not to be silly. Mr Ticker was only a chicken farmer; what could he do to him?

Daniel reached the door of the first shed. There was nobody to be seen: the high door was bolted and barred and above it was another notice saying NO ENTRY.

He walked over to the second building. Here the door was open a crack. He slipped inside.

The light was poor and at first, mercifully, Daniel could scarcely see. Only the smell hit him instantly: a truly awful smell of sickness and rottenness and decay.

Then came the sounds: half-strangled cries, desperate squawks . . .

But now his eyes were becoming used to the gloom. He could make out rows and rows of wire cages piled from floor to ceiling on either side of narrow concrete corridors that seemed to stretch away for miles.

And he could see what was inside the cages. Not one chicken, but two, packed so close together that they could hardly turn their heads or move. Unspeakable things were happening in those cages. In one, a bird had caught its throat in the wire and choked; in another, a chicken driven mad by overcrowding was trying to peck out its neighbour's eyes. There were cages in which one bird lay dead while the other was pressed against its corpse. And yet somehow, unbelievably, the wretched creatures went on laying eggs – large brown eggs which rolled on to the shelf below, ready to be driven to Wellbridge Market and make Ralph Ticker rich.

Daniel was turning back, knowing he'd be sick if he stayed any longer, when he heard voices at the far end of the shed.

'There's another seventeen birds died in the night, Mr Ticker.'

'Well, mince 'em up, feed them to the rest and burn the feathers out at the back.'

'I don't like to, sir. People have been complaining about the smell. If they call the RSPCA . . .'

'They won't.' And then: 'Who's that up there? Why, it's a bloomin' kid!'

Daniel tried to run for the entrance, but it was too late. Mr Ticker pulled down a switch and the building was flooded with light. There was wild clucking from the hens and then the chicken farmer, followed by his assistant, came running up the aisle. Then a hand banged down on Daniel's shoulder and Mr Ticker's red face, with its bulbous nose, was thrust into the boy's.

'What the *devil* are you doing in here?'

'I was . . . just . . . looking.' Mr Ticker was shaking him so hard that Daniel could scarcely get out the words.

'Did you see the notice? Did you see where it says KEEP OUT?' With each question he shook Daniel again. 'You were snooping, weren't you? You were spying. Well, let me tell you, if you say one word about this place to anyone, I'll get you. I'll get your mother too. I've got people everywhere. People who throw acid, people with guns . . . Got it?'

60

He pushed Daniel forward and the boy stumbled out and ran over the bridge of wooden planks, across the fields . . . ran, panting, for the safety of the station.

And Ralph Ticker looked after him with narrowed eyes.

'It's no good, sir,' said the assistant when Daniel was out of sight. 'Even if the kid keeps quiet, they're beginning to talk in the village.'

Ticker said nothing. Twice before, the inspectors of the RSPCA, those snooping Do-Gooders, had closed down his chicken farms. Once in Cornwall, once in Yorkshire – and the second time he'd been fined two hundred pounds. But what was two hundred pounds – chicken feed, thought Ticker, grinning at his own joke. Each time he'd made a whopping profit before they got wise to him.

'Time to move on, Bert,' he said. 'Scotland this time, I think. You know what to do.'

'But, Mr Ticker, there's four thousand chickens here. I can't chop the heads off—'

'Oh, I think you can, Bert. Yes, really I think you can.'

'You've got to do something,' said Daniel, trying not to cry into the 'nice cup of tea' which Heckie had brewed him. 'You've got to turn him into a chicken himself and force him into one of those cages and—'

'Now, Daniel,' said Heckie severely, 'how many times have I told you that the second someone becomes a chicken he is not a wicked chicken, he is a chicken who needs only the best? And anyway, the

61

zoo doesn't want a chicken, what the zoo wants is an okapi. Now drink up and leave everything to me.'

The next day, without saying anything to the children, Heckie called the wizards and witches to a meeting. She had made a map of the Tritlington Poultry Unit from Daniel's description and was feeling important, like Napoleon.

'Now you all understand exactly what you have to do?' she asked.

'I'm to flush him out of the building,' said the cheese wizard gloomily. He was not looking forward at all to changing Mr Ticker into an okapi. He had never seen an okapi and didn't know if he would like it if he did, and he couldn't remember a single spell for flushing anybody out of anything at all.

'And I'm to lure him into the field with my beauty,' said Madame Rosalia, fluttering her false eyelashes which were made of spider's legs.

Heckie frowned. 'I didn't say anything about luring. What I said was, I want him in the field in front of the shed because I shall need space to work in. Boris will take you all down in the van and park it across the drive so that Ticker can't escape in his car. And you, Frieda, must stop him crossing the bridge. If he makes a dash for the station, we're done for.'

'How?' said the garden witch. 'How do I stop him?'

'How? Good heavens, woman, you're a witch. Root him to the ground. Wrap his legs in ivy. Just stop him!'

Frieda scratched her head and Heckie reached

irritably for the garden shears. Really, having to deal with witches of such poor quality was hard.

'But what about you?' asked Madame Rosalia. 'How are you going to get there?'

Heckie simpered. 'I shall descend from On High!'

'Eh?'

'I shall float down in one of Boris's hot air balloons,' said Heckie, waving a hand at the mechanical wizard and feeling more like Napoleon than ever. 'And remember, not a word to the children till it's all over. We wizards and witches may be bullet-proof, but not the children.'

Nobody liked the sound of this at all. It was so long since any of them had done any proper magic that they had no idea whether they were bullet-proof or not.

But the cheese wizard had other worries too. 'Do they bite?' he asked, as he shuffled with the others to the door.

'Do what bite?'

'Those okapi things. I just wondered.'

Ralph Ticker was standing by the great hole he'd bulldozed the day before on the waste ground behind the sheds. He was waiting for Bert to come and chop off the heads of the birds and bury them. Once the hole was covered, there'd be nothing to show those snoopy RSPCA people that there'd ever been hens in the place, and he'd be safely away over the border.

Only where was Bert? He was late. Ticker's Porsche was parked in the drive, his case was packed – but he certainly wasn't going to kill four thousand chickens by himself.

What Ralph Ticker didn't know was that Bert had already done a bunk. He was sick of cutting the heads off chickens for peanuts and he was sick of Ticker. While his employer waited by the death pit, Bert was on the pier at Brighton, playing the fruit-machines.

The wizards and witches, meanwhile, were driving down to Tritlington. It was an uncomfortable journey. They had to sit crowded together on the bench seat in the front because the van had been got ready for the okapi, with padding on the walls and lots of straw. Boris, who had an unhappy nature like most Russians, was worried about Heckie's hot air balloon. She had asked for a blue one to match the sky and he'd let her have it before he remembered that that was the one he'd been doing experiments on. Boris had always been sure one could invent a hot air balloon that flew on the hot air talked by politicians, but so far he hadn't managed it – and now he couldn't remember whether he'd put enough fuel back in the machine.

By the time they reached the poultry unit, everyone was feeling ill-tempered and car-sick. As for Mr Gurgle, he wasn't just feeling sick, he was feeling extremely frightened. But he had said he would flush Mr Ticker out of the poultry shed, and flush he would. Trying desperately to remember some useful spells, Mr Gurgle crept towards the door.

'Coo-ee!' he called. 'I see you!'

But he didn't, at first, see anything. He was very short-sighted and the shed was almost dark. Groping his way forward, he felt for his spectacles and put them on – but this was a mistake. Now he *could* see.

Mr Gurgle was not fond of chickens and had thought he didn't mind what happened to them, but he was wrong. As he reeled from cage to cage, his stomach heaved and sweat broke out on his forehead. Stumbling on, his foot hit a zinc bucket with a crack like a pistol shot – and a large black rat, carrying a chewed chicken leg, scurried across his path.

It was too much. Mr Gurgle gave a cry of terror and fainted clean away.

After this, things happened quickly, but not exactly the way Heckie had planned.

Ralph Ticker heard the pistol shot, rushed into the shed – and saw a dead man! A gang fighting it out in his buildings! White with fear, he ran to the entrance, meaning to make a dash for his car. But a van was slewed across the road and in it, a man with a long, cruel face. Ticker doubled back – and straight into the arms of a ghastly gangster's moll!

'Come into the field, you dear man,' leered Madame Rosalia. She fluttered her eyelashes so hard that they came off, and the chicken farmer, seeing what he thought was a Black Widow Spider on his trousers, shrieked and bolted for the bridge.

'You can't come by! Not here you can't!'

Ticker stopped dead. A talking bush. A bush with a leafy top, but two fat pink legs – legs which ended in large green Wellington boots. But if Ticker was terrified of a bush in wellies, he was even more frightened of the gangsters behind him. He pushed the bush violently to one side and set off across the bridge.

The station was ahead now, and safety.

Only what was that thing above him? A hot air balloon – and coming down very fast. Dangerously fast. It was going to land on top of him!

Ticker crouched down on the planks, trying to cover his head with his hands. And then, just as it seemed certain that he would be squashed flat, the balloon veered to one side – and landed with a gigantic splash in the water!

'Ha, ha, ha!' laughed Ticker, forgetting to run. He was the sort of man who loved to see people in trouble.

But even as he leant over and jeered, something was coming up behind him. A bush in boots, which now lifted one leg and kicked him very hard on the backside.

'Whoosh! Phlup! Guggle!' spluttered the chicken farmer as he landed in the deep and icy water.

And then a voice, close by, in the river. A kind voice like a nice nannie's. 'Don't worry,' it said. 'I'll help you. I'll hold you. Just keep calm because I'm swimming right up to you and I'm going to hold you *very tight*!'

The journey back was not a happy one. Mr Gurgle still felt faint and was lying down in the straw they had put down for the okapi. Boris was full of gloom and guilt because of what had happened to the air balloon, and Frieda's left foot was cold.

'All right, that's *enough*,' snapped Heckie. She was soaking wet, but what she was worrying about was what was in Frieda's Wellington boot which she was holding carefully on her lap. She had filled it to the brim with water, but even the best wellies leak a little, and if the poor dear fish that swam inside it should dry out and die before they reached Wellbridge, she would never forgive herself. 'So Frieda's foot is cold, so Rosalia's lost her eyelashes, so you wanted an okapi. I've told you, I can't go struggling about in the water with a kind of giraffe. They're poor swimmers, giraffes – everyone says so.'

'We understand that,' said Madame Rosalia. 'No one's making a fuss because you turned Mr Ticker into a fish. What we don't understand is why you didn't leave him where he was.'

'I told you why,' said Heckie irritably. 'Because the river's polluted. No fish could last in it for more than a couple of days.'

'Well, I can't see that it matters. After what he did to those chickens . . .'

Heckie opened her mouth and shut it again. She was absolutely sick of explaining to people that the second someone was a fish, he was not a wicked fish or a fish who had tortured chickens, he was simply a fish.

Everything had gone well, really. She had phoned the RSPCA and they'd promised to send some men at once to see to the hens, and Ralph Ticker would never harm a living thing again. But it wasn't much fun sharing adventures with these moaners and grumblers. If she'd had her old friend with her, how different it would all have been!

'Oh, where are you, Dora?' sighed Heckie, clutching her watery boot.

# Chapter Ten

Dora was sitting on an upturned chamberpot in the back of a swaying furniture lorry. Round her were all the things she had brought from Kidchester: her bed, her kitchen table and chairs, her work bench and her tools.

She had decided to move to the outskirts of Wellbridge, where a nice garden statue business had come up for sale, and she was doing it in secret. She hadn't said a word to Heckie or to anyone she knew. After all, it might be that Heckie was going to be cross with her for ever. On the other hand, if they lived in the same city, even at opposite ends of it, they just could meet by accident and then . . .

The lorry lurched round the corner and Dora clutched the metal jam pan which contained her hat. The hat wasn't well at all – the overfeeding had caused the snakes to start shedding their skins. If she wore it now, people would think she had the most awful dandruff.

'Should I put it on a diet?' wondered poor Dora as the lorry ground up the hill past Wellbridge prison. But what sort of a diet was best for hats? It was Heckie who knew about animals. 'Come to that, I ought to go on a diet myself.'

It was true that Dora, who had never been thin, was now definitely overweight. People who are lonely often eat too much and Dora had really been stuffing herself. Muscles, of course, are important for stonework, but fat is another thing.

Nothing had gone well for the stone witch in Kidchester. She'd managed to do some good all right: Dr Franklin, the one who'd done the awful experiments on dogs, really did look very nice by the fountain in the middle of the shopping centre, and she'd found a comfortable spot for a swindler who'd gone off with the life savings of a lot of poor people. He stood between two pillars in front of the Pensions Office, where the starlings were enjoying him. But Kidchester wasn't pretty like Wellbridge . . .

No, I'm lying, thought Dora. It's because I miss Heckie that I'm moving. It's because I miss my friend.

They bumped over some old tram lines and from the wardrobe, pushed against one wall, there came a worried bleat.

'Don't chop down the wardrobe,' begged the ghost. 'Don't chop—'

'I'm not *going* to chop it down!' said Dora, for the hundredth time. 'It's trees they chop down and *you're not in a tree*!'

They had passed the prison and the football ground. Not much further to go . . .

Well, I've done it now, thought Dora. And even if I don't meet Heckie, I can still do some good here. There must be lots of wicked people left in Wellbridge even after Heckie's finished with the place. But oh, if only I met her. If only we became friends again!

The lorry stopped at the lights. Just a few metres away, facing in the other direction, was a blue van with sealed windows. Inside it sat Heckie, holding the Wellington boot with the fish in it.

Oh, if only Dora was here, she was thinking just at that moment. If only I had her to help me instead of these useless moaners.

Then the lights changed. The vans moved forward – and neither of the witches knew how close to each other they had been.

# Chapter Eleven

Daniel never quarrelled with Sumi. She was so gentle and so sensible that he wouldn't have known how to begin. But after Ralph Ticker was changed, they came as close to quarrelling as they had ever done.

'Well, I still don't think it's right,' she said. 'I think it's dangerous changing people into animals and I don't think Heckie should do it.'

They were in her parents' grocery shop, parcelling up black-eyed beans, and Daniel was so cross he let the beans spill from his shovel way past the correct weight.

'I suppose you think it's right to torture four thousand chickens and then plan to murder them in cold blood.'

'No, I don't. You know I don't. But he could have been sent to prison and—'

'He couldn't,' said Daniel angrily. 'The RSPCA kept trying and all he got was a measly fine. And anyway, I don't see that it's so terrible being an unusual fish. Being an ordinary fish might be, but he isn't. People have been coming from all over the country to find out what he is, and I should think it's very exciting.'

This was true. The fish that Heckie had left in a tank by the West Gate of the zoo labelled: ANOTHER

PRESENT FROM A WELL WISHER had really brought the scientists running.

Sumi didn't say any more. She knew how Daniel felt about Heckie, and she knew why. If you had a mother who had written seven books about The Meaning of Meaning and had no time for you, you might well turn to a warm-hearted witch for the love you didn't get at home.

And quite soon they had something more to worry them than whether Ralph Ticker did, or did not, like being an unusual fish.

Although she was so busy Doing Good, Heckie never forgot her pet shop. Since she knew so much about animals, all the rabbits and guinea pigs she sold were healthy, so she made quite a lot of money. At first she had kept this money in her mattress, but she was worried that the mice who lived there would nibble it and this would be bad for them.

'Mice have very tender stomachs,' she told the children. 'Not everyone knows that, but it's true.'

So she went to the bank and signed a lot of papers and after that, every Friday afternoon, she paid in her takings.

Heckie liked going to the bank. She enjoyed chatting with the other shopkeepers and the people in the queue. It made her feel ordinary and that is a thing that witches do not often feel.

On the particular Friday when something unexpected happened at the bank, Heckie found herself standing beside a tall and very distinguished-looking man with a Roman nose, dark eyes set very close together, and a little beard like goats have. He wore a black coat with a fur collar and carried an ivory cane, and Heckie thought she had never seen anyone more handsome. She didn't approve of the fur collar, but there was always the hope that the raccoon it was made of had died in his sleep, and no one is perfect. So she gave him a beaming smile, showing all her large and sticking out teeth, and when he got to the counter, she listened carefully as the clerk said: 'Good morning, Mr Knacksap,' and thought what an unusual name Knacksap was and how well it suited him.

Mr Knacksap wasn't putting money into the bank, he was taking it out, and as she waited, she squinted over his shoulder at his cheque-book and saw that his initial was L. Did that stand for Lucien or Lancelot or Lovelace? Such an elegant man was sure to have an unusual name.

Mr Knacksap took his money and Heckie smiled at him again, but he didn't smile back. Then it was her turn. She had just put her paying-in book down on the counter, when the door burst open and a masked man rushed into the bank, waving a sawn-off shotgun.

'Everybody on the floor!' he shouted to the people in the queue.

Everybody got down at once, even Heckie who had become very excited. She had seen bank robbers on the telly, but never in real life. This one looked a bit thin and she thought he might have a hungry wife and children at home, or perhaps he was going to give the money to the poor like Robin Hood.

'Anyone who moves, gets it,' the robber went on, and strode to the counter. Outside, Heckie could see a van parked alongside the kerb, and a fierce-looking man inside. The getaway car! Really, it was just like the telly!

Mr Knacksap, lying on the floor beside Heckie, did not seem to be excited at all. He looked quite green and his beautiful bowler hat had rolled away. Heckie wanted to comfort him, but she thought it was best to keep quiet till the robber had gone.

'Come on, hand it over. The lot! And hurry!' barked the robber.

Heckie squinted up and saw a little fat cashier run up to the grille with wads of bank-notes, and start pushing them through. 'Don't shoot!' he kept saying, 'Don't shoot!' The other cashiers were huddled together at the back – all except one girl. A very young girl with long blonde hair who looked as though she had only just left school. She was edging her way carefully forward to where the alarm bell was. She had almost reached it . . .

The next second there was a blast from the shotgun, a scream . . . and the blonde girl fell across her desk with blood streaming from her shoulder.

Up to now, Heckie had just been interested. Of course it was wrong to rob banks, but after all if there was one thing banks had plenty of, it was money.

But now she lost her temper. Her eyes narrowed, her knuckle throbbed, she kicked off her shoe. The robber, meanwhile, had turned away from the counter. He felt in his pocket and lobbed a metal canister on to the floor where the people were lying. It was a smoke bomb, and as the choking fumes spread through the room, he made for the door.

At least he started off. But a hand had fastened round his ankle . . . a hand like a steel trap. He raised his gun, ready to shoot . . . but he didn't seem to have arms any more . . . he didn't seem to have . . . anything.

No one else saw. As they groped and struggled to the exit, they thought that the robber had escaped. But Mr Knacksap, lying beside Heckie, had seen. He had seen the robber's shape become dim . . . become wavery . . . shrink almost to nothing. And then re-form in the shape of a small brown mouse which scampered over to the wall panelling – and was gone!

Mr Knacksap's Christian name was not Lancelot or Lucien, it was Lionel, and the raccoon on his collar had not died in its sleep because Mr Knacksap was a furrier. He owned a shop in Market Square where he sold fur coats and he had a workshop in the basement and a store-room where he kept the skins of dead animals ready to be made up into coats or sold to other furriers at a profit.

The shop was called Knacksap and Knacksap, but the first Knacksap, who had been Mr Knacksap's father, was now dead. The old man had been a good craftsman and had made very beautiful coats which ladies had paid good money for, because in those days people did not think it was cruel to kill an animal simply for its skin and there were not so many other ways of keeping warm. But his son, Lionel Knacksap, was not a good craftsman. His coats were badly made, and at the time he took over, people were beginning to ask annoying questions before they bought fur coats. They wanted to know

75

how the animals had been killed – had they suffered at all, and were they rare; because if so they didn't want to wear them.

So Mr Knacksap found himself getting poorer and poorer, and as he was a man who had expensive tastes, he didn't like this at all. In the basement he had kept two ladies who made coats for him. Now he sacked them and started doing business with very dubious people. These were men who came at night and talked to him in the shop with the shutters closed and they wanted him to get skins for them that were no longer allowed to be sold in England: the skins of Sumatran tigers or jaguars from the Amazon – beautiful animals that were almost extinct. They were willing to pay thousands of pounds for pelts like that because there were always vain or ridiculous people who would do anything to lie on a tiger skin or wear a coat like no other in the world. But it wasn't easy to get hold of such skins. Mr Knacksap was finding it very hard to supply his customers and he had been getting into debt.

And then he saw Heckie fasten her hands round the bank robber's ankle and realized that he had been lying next to a very powerful witch. A witch who could change people into animals. But any animal? Mr Knacksap meant to find out.

# Chapter Twelve

Heckie was worrying about the mouse. Suppose they set mouse-traps in the bank and it got caught?

'Or killed,' she said, looking desperate. 'Imagine it! An animal I produced, lying dead! I had no time to think, you see, but that's no excuse.'

'I'm sure they don't use traps,' said Daniel. 'I've never seen a mouse-trap in a bank.'

'It'll be perfectly happy behind the panelling, eating the crumbs from the cashier's sandwiches,' said Sumi.

But it was hard to comfort Heckie. Dora had known how to do it; she'd just told Heckie to shut up and not be so daft, but the children couldn't do that, and Heckie went on pacing up and down and saying that if anybody she'd changed into an animal got hurt, she'd never know another moment's happiness again.

'Why don't we take the dragworm for a walk?' said Joe, who was used to dealing with gorillas when they went over the top. 'Then you can go to the bank and *ask* about mouse-traps.'

Heckie thought this was a good idea – she wanted to enquire anyway about the girl who'd been shot in the shoulder. As for the dragworm, he only had to hear the word 'walk' and he was already inside the tartan shopping basket on wheels. It fitted him just like a house with a roof and he was never happier than when he was rattling and bumping through the streets of Wellbridge.

When they had gone, Heckie went to change her batskin robe for something more suitable, but she never got to the bank, for just then the doorbell rang.

Out in the hall, holding a bunch of flowers, stood the tall, distinguished man that Heckie had seen in the bank.

'Forgive me for calling,' he said. 'My name is Knacksap. Lionel Knacksap. May I come in?'

Mr Knacksap was wearing his dark coat with the raccoon collar and his bowler hat, and smelled strongly of a toilet water called Male.

'Yes, please do.' Heckie was quite overcome. 'I was just going to . . . change.'

'You look delightful as you are,' said Mr Knacksap in an oily voice, and handed her the flowers which he had stolen from the garden of an old lady who was blind. 'I came to congratulate you. I saw, you see. I saw what you did in the bank.' And as Heckie frowned: 'But don't worry, Miss . . . er . . . Tenbury-Smith. Your secret is safe with me.'

Heckie now offered him a cup of tea. This time she put in three tea-bags because she had never been alone before with such a handsome gentleman, but Mr Knacksap said that was just how he liked it.

'Tell me,' he said, resting his cup genteelly on his knee. 'Can you turn people into any kind of animal? Or only little things like mice?'

'Oh, yes, pretty well any animal,' said Heckie,

looking modest. 'But of course I have to think of what will happen to it afterwards.'

Mr Knacksap's eyes glittered with excitement. 'Could you, for example, could you . . . say . . . turn someone into a tiger? A large tiger?'

Heckie nodded. 'I'd have to make sure they wanted a tiger in the zoo.'

She then went on to tell the furrier of her plans for making Wellbridge a better place. 'I have such wonderful helpers. Wizards and witches – and children. The children in particular! And a most wonderful familiar – a dragworm. He's just out for a walk, but you must meet him. He's a wickedness detector and he can sniff out even the tiniest bit of evil!'

Mr Knacksap didn't like the sound of that at all. 'I'm afraid I'm completely allergic to dragons . . . and . . . er, worms. What I mean is, I can't bear to be in the same room. When I was small, I had asthma, you see; I couldn't get my breath, and the doctors told me that if I went near anything like . . . the thing you have described, I would simply choke to death.'

Heckie was very disappointed. She had set her heart on showing the dragworm to this attractive man. But of course the idea of Lionel Knacksap choking to death was too horrible to think about.

Mr Knacksap, in the meantime, was doing sums in his head. A tiger skin fetched over two thousand pounds. Even after he'd paid someone to kill and skin the beast, there'd be a nice profit. And plenty more where that came from: ocelots, jaguars, lynx . . . All he had to do was butter up this frumpy witch.

'Dear Miss Tenbury-Smith—'

'Heckie. Please call me Heckie.'

Mr Knacksap gulped. 'Dear Heckie – I wonder if you would care to have dinner with me next Saturday? At the Trocadero at eight o'clock?'

'How do I look?' asked Heckie, and Sumi and Daniel said she looked very nice.

This was true. Heckie had gone to Madame Rosalia for advice about what to wear for her night out with the furrier, but she had made it clear that she wanted to be tastefully dressed.

'I may be a witch,' Heckie had said to Madame Rosalia, 'but I am also a woman.'

So she had decided not to wear black whiskers on her chin, or a blue tooth, and just three blackheads – more enlarged pores, really – on the end of her nose. And her dress was tasteful too – a black sheath embroidered all over with small green toads.

'My shoes pinch,' said Heckie, but there was nothing to be done about that. Heckie's Toe of Transformation always hurt when she bought new shoes.

Mr Knacksap had booked a table by the window and ordered a three-course meal. He hated spending money, but he knew that if he was going to get the witch to do what he wanted, he'd have to make a splash for once. The Trocadero was very smart, with gleaming white tablecloths and a man playing sloppy music on the piano, but the dinner didn't get off to a very good start.

The trouble began with a beetle that was crawling

80

about in the centre of a rose in a cut glass vase on the table. Heckie thought the beetle did not look well and she asked the waiter if he'd mind putting it out in the garden, if possible near a cowpat.

'It's a dung beetle, you see,' she told him, 'so it really cannot be happy on this rose.'

Then the starter came and it was shrimps in mayonnaise.

'Is there anything wrong?' asked Mr Knacksap. 'They look nice and pink to me.'

'Yes,' said Heckie faintly. 'But you see, shrimps aren't meant to be pink. They're meant to be a sort of grey. If they're pink they're dead.'

'Well, we could hardly eat them if they weren't,' said Mr Knacksap, but he had to keep on the right side of Heckie so he sent them back and ordered vegetable soup.

After the shrimps came some meat in a brown sauce and when Heckie saw it, she turned quite pale.

'*Now* what's the matter?' asked Mr Knacksap. 'Those are pheasant breasts done in wine.'

'I know they're pheasant breasts,' said Heckie faintly. 'But you see eating them would be . . . well, like eating a friend.' And as Mr Knacksap frowned at her: 'You must know what I mean. Think of a friend of yours. Any friend.'

Mr Knacksap tried to think of a friend he had had. 'There was a boy called Marvin Minor at my prep school. He used to lend me his roller skates.'

'Well, now you see,' said Heckie. 'Imagine you were served slices of Marvin Minor's chest in wine sauce. How would you feel?'

But even now, Mr Knacksap kept his temper. The

81

pheasant breasts were taken away and Heckie was given a mushroom omelette instead. And there was no fuss over the pudding. Even Heckie didn't think that caramel custard was like swallowing a friend.

By now they had drunk quite a lot of wine and Mr Knacksap was ready to come to the point.

'I have a favour to ask you,' he said, leaning across the table and fixing Heckie with his piercing eyes. 'A great favour!'

Heckie looked down at the tablecloth and tried to flutter her eyelashes like she had seen Madame Rosalia do. 'Yes?' she said shyly.

'I want you to make a tiger for me. I want you to change the next wicked person you see into a tiger. A male tiger – and large.'

'Well, I will if you like, Lionel,' said Heckie (because she had been told to use his Christian name). 'But are you sure you can manage it? They're tricky things to look after, the big cats.'

'It's not for me personally – I wouldn't ask you anything for myself,' said Mr Knacksap soupily. 'It's for a friend of mine. An aristocrat. A lord.'

'Oh, really?'

Everyone is a bit impressed by lords, and Heckie was no exception.

'Yes. The poor man was left a great castle . . . I don't like to talk about him because he's very shy, but you'd know the name if I told you. But it's in a very bad state – loose tiles on the roof, dry rot, all that kind of thing. So he's started a safari park to bring in the trippers and help him get enough money to do repairs. But what the safari park really needs is a tiger.'

'Well, if you're sure he'd care for it properly.'

'It would live like a prince,' said Mr Knacksap. 'A heated house, a huge enclosure, children to come and photograph it. And my friend would be so happy.'

Heckie stirred her coffee. 'All right, then. Mind you, one can't be absolutely certain with this kind of magic. Sometimes things sort of happen by themselves. There was an animal witch in Germany who kept being overcome by hippopotamuses. Whatever she tried to turn people into, they always came out as hippos.'

Mr Knacksap didn't like the sound of that. No one wore coats made of hippopotamus skins. 'I'm sure that wouldn't happen to you, dear Heckie,' he said. 'You're such a powerful witch. I knew the moment I saw you.'

As soon as he got back to his shop that evening, Mr Knacksap telephoned a man he knew in Manchester. 'Is that you, Ferguson?'

'Yes, it's me.'

'Well, listen; I've got you your tiger skin. A full-grown male.'

'Go on. You're kidding.'

'No, I'm not. I take it the Arkle woman still wants one?'

'You bet she does. She's upped the price to two and a half thousand.'

Gertrude Arkle was married to a chain-store millionaire and had set her heart on a tiger skin to put on her bedroom floor. She wanted to lie on it in silk pyjamas like she had seen film stars do in pictures of the olden days. And the more Mr Arkle told

her that she couldn't have one because it was illegal
to import them, the more she wanted one.

'All right, then,' said Mr Knacksap. 'I'll give you
a call when it's ready.'

# Chapter Thirteen

For nearly three weeks after Heckie had dinner with Mr Knacksap at the Trocadero, life went on much as usual. Heckie was still trying to get the dragworm to speak. She told him stories and repeated simple words to him, but though he was always polite and listened to everything she said, it didn't seem as though he was ever going to talk. In other ways, though, he was learning all the time. He could turn the bath tap on now with his front claws, and put in the plug, and he didn't have to think nearly so long about which of his feet was which. Heckie had worried, as the days grew warmer, that he might become unsettled. Chinese dragons usually fly up to heaven in the spring and she would have missed him horribly if he had done so, but he stayed where he was.

Still, things were not quite the same as before and this was because of Mr Knacksap. The furrier never came to the flat because of the dragworm, but the children had seen him in the street and they didn't like what they saw. They thought he looked thoroughly creepy and unreliable and they couldn't understand why Heckie went out with him.

The children weren't the only ones to be worried. The cheese wizard's shop was next door to the furrier's and he knew quite a lot about Mr

Knacksap. Daniel had met him in the street and been asked in to see a Stilton that could walk at least half a metre.

'And it's not maggots, either; it's magic,' said Mr Gurgle, beaming at the cheese as it struggled across the floor. But afterwards he became serious. 'I don't like the way that fellow's paying court to Heckie,' he said. 'He's got a bad name in the trade. Up to his eyebrows in debt – and the way he treated those sewing women who worked for him was a scandal. If she marries him, she'll—'

'Oh, but she couldn't! She *couldn't*!' cried Daniel, looking completely stricken.

'Well, I don't suppose she will. But she's all heart and no head, that witch. Just you keep an eye on her.'

But this was easier said than done. Mr Knacksap was careful always to see Heckie away from the shop. Since he hated spending money, he took her on picnics. Heckie brought the food so it didn't cost him anything, and all he brought was a towel to sit on because he didn't like nature and was fussy about his trousers.

Mr Knacksap realized that it was no good pretending that he wasn't a furrier – after all, his shop was in Market Square for everyone to see. So he told Heckie a lot of lies about the coats he sold.

'That beaver cape in my window was made by a tribe of North American Indians who worship beavers. They sing to them and feed them on pine nuts and take them to sleep with them in their wigwams so that they live for years and years and years. And then when they pass on – the beavers, I mean

86

– the Indians make them into coats so that they won't be forgotten.'

'Oh, Li-Li, that's wonderful,' said Heckie, feasting her eyes on Mr Knacksap as they sat on a rock high above the Wellbridge gas works.

'And the stoats I use come from an organic stoat farm in Sweden. They shave the animals and sew the fur on to canvas so that it looks like a pelt, but it isn't. Only when it's warm, they shave them; no stoat is ever allowed to get chilled.'

So Heckie's last doubts were gone. Not only was Mr Knacksap the handsomest man she had ever seen, but he was kind to animals. But inside, Mr Knacksap was seething. Three weeks and not a sign of a tiger! How long was he supposed to go on buttering up this ridiculous witch?

Sumi had put her three little brothers to bed. She had sung to them and played Three Little Pigs Go To Market with the fat toes of the youngest, and now they were drowsy and quiet.

Down in the shop, her mother was putting the CLOSED sign across the door and her father was emptying the till.

'You're closing early?' she asked in the Punjabi they always spoke when they were alone. It was only eight thirty, and her parents often served customers till late at night.

Her mother nodded. She looked tired and her eyes were swollen.

'Is anything wrong?' Sumi adored her parents and her voice was sharp with anxiety.

'No, no, nothing.' Her mother managed a smile. 'We're just going to have an early night.'

But there was something wrong. Sumi knew from the way her parents went upstairs, walking very close together, their shoulders almost touching. They weren't like the parents of her schoolfriends, kissing and hugging in front of everyone. They were dignified and shy, but tonight they needed to be very close.

Sumi went to bed, but she couldn't sleep. And her mother and father couldn't sleep either. She heard their voices, low and sad, going on and on. After a while she got up and crept to the door. If there was trouble in the family she wanted to know and help.

'Shall we tell Sumi? We'll keep the boys indoors, but she'll have to have protection when she goes to school. I don't want her going out of the house while he's here with his thugs. And we must get metal shutters for the windows.'

'Expensive . . .' Her father sounded worried.

'Expensive? What does that matter? We can borrow. You know what happened to Ved . . . you saw my sister's face when they brought him home, and you talk about expensive!'

Back in her room, Sumi began to shiver. It was a warm night, but she couldn't stop trembling. For she knew what had happened to Ved. She knew what was making her parents so afraid.

Oh, what shall I do? thought Sumi. Whatever shall I do?

Heckie was clearing away her breakfast when Sumi rang the doorbell of the flat. She was pleased to see her – people were always pleased to see Sumi – but worried that she'd be late for school.

'It doesn't matter if I am,' said Sumi – and then Heckie knew that there was something seriously wrong because Sumi really loved school.

'What is it, dear?'

So then Sumi told her. 'A man is coming to Wellbridge; an absolutely terrible man. He's called Max Swinton and he's the leader of something called the White Avengers.'

Heckie frowned. 'Those racist thugs who go round bashing up people?'

'Yes. And it's Swinton that leads them on. He's worse than Hitler. They shout things that don't sound so terrible, like BRITISH FOR THE BRITISH, but by British they only mean people with white skins and they don't care what they do to the . . . others.' She stopped to blow her nose. 'I have this cousin in London. Ved, he's called. He was a violinist – he won a scholarship to music college when he was fifteen. He was coming home alone after a concert when a gang of Swinton's thugs got hold of him. We thought he wouldn't live at first, he was so badly hurt. But he did live. He's alive. Only his hands . . . When they saw the violin, they jumped on his hands . . .'

Sumi gulped and groped for her handkerchief, and Heckie put her arms round her and waited till she could go on.

Then she lifted her head and said what she had come to say. 'I told Daniel that I didn't think it was right to turn people into animals, but I've changed

89

my mind. Please, Heckie ... please will you turn Max Swinton into absolutely *anything*.'

Swinton's picture was in the next day's paper. The dragworm wouldn't stay in the same room with it and went to have a bath while Heckie and Daniel studied his face.

'He looks like a pig,' said Daniel.

'No, he doesn't,' said Heckie firmly. 'Pigs may have small eyes, but they are *intelligent* eyes, and if they're fat, it's a firm fatness, not wobbly.'

Swinton was coming to Wellbridge on the following Monday, in a motorcade, to make speeches. The police had broken up Swinton's rallies before; he had even been to prison, but never long enough to keep him and his followers off the streets.

'He's staying at the Queen's Hotel, I see,' said Heckie. 'Didn't you say you had a friend whose mother worked there?'

'Yes, I did. Henry, he's called. He's really nice, and his older brother has just started as a bell-boy. I'm sure he'd help us. Henry's black, I expect he feels just like Sumi does about the Avengers.'

The Queen's Hotel was very grand. It stood on the edge of the park with its pretty flower-beds and statues, and the pond where Heckie had found the duck that didn't want to live. Towers and turrets burst from the roof of the hotel and flags blew in the wind, and there were awnings and waiters rushing about and a whole army of chambermaids.

'So you think Henry can be trusted? That he can keep a secret?'

'Yes, I do.'

'Good. Then I suggest you go and find him straight away and bring him here.'

Mr Knacksap read Heckie's note and his eyes glittered with greed. A tiger at last! He was to arrange for a closed horse box and a driver, and get hold of a wire tunnel of the kind that circus trainers use to lead animals into the ring.

'Because we don't want the poor dear creature getting scared and muddled,' Heckie had written.

Henry's brother was going to meet her in the park at daybreak with the key to Max Swinton's room and a chambermaid's uniform belonging to his mother.

'Then I'll slip into his room with his early morning tea and change him. By great good luck, he's got a downstairs room so you'll be able to park the horse box almost under his window. Remember to have a nice raw steak ready for him. Tigers can get very hungry when they're on the road.'

Oh, yes, the brute would find a steak all right, thought Mr Knacksap. A drugged steak which would knock him out, then a clean shot between the eyes so as to make the smallest possible hole in the pelt – and off to be skinned! Mr Knacksap had even arranged for a man who made pet food to take the carcass!

Two thousand pounds clear! Alone in his shop, the furrier smiled and rubbed his hands.

Heckie was up before it was light, feeling extremely happy. She had enjoyed changing Mrs Winneypeg and the chicken farmer, but in ridding the world of Max Swinton she was doing more good than she had ever done before *and* giving her Li-Li the tiger he wanted so much for his friend!

Daniel was waiting for her at the gates of the park. She had promised he could come just till she met Henry's brother, Clem. But no sooner had Daniel run up to her, than Mr Knacksap came round the corner in his bowler hat and fur-collared coat.

'Lionel! I didn't expect you! Why aren't you with the horse box?'

'I just wanted to see you safely into the hotel, dear,' said the furrier.

But what Mr Knacksap really wanted was to make sure that Heckie didn't change her mind or go all soft. One thing he couldn't be doing with was a hippopotamus.

Daniel wasn't at all pleased to see the furrier, but he had to be polite and together they walked past flower-beds and the pond, and between smooth lawns that were still wet with dew.

Clem had kept his promise. He was waiting by the fountain with the key and the uniform.

'Everything's okay,' he whispered. 'He's in room seventeen like I said.'

Heckie thanked him and they waited while he ran back to the hotel where all the guests still slept. Then they followed him, making their way along a gravel path between neatly clipped hedges.

'Funny, there's a new statue,' said Mr Knacksap, pointing with his cane.

'Yes, there is,' said Daniel.

Heckie had been thinking of the job ahead of her. Now she looked up, stopped, took a step towards the statue . . .

And another . . .

Then she put back her head and screamed.

Daniel reached her first. 'What is it?' he gasped. 'What's the matter?'

But Heckie couldn't speak. She just pointed at the statue with a hand which shook as if she had a dreadful fever.

'It's Dora,' she managed to bring out. 'Dora Mayberry did it. She's betrayed me, she's cheated me! She's done me out of my triumph! This is her work. I'd know it anywhere!'

Daniel went right up to the statue – and then he understood.

It was Max Swinton who stood there, carefully mounted on a marble slab. Max Swinton's mean little eyes, his silly moustache, his fat chin, were all there in stone. His trousers, tight over his straining thighs, his bulging beer belly, the Avenger's badge . . . all were there, for ever and ever, caught in white marble now touched by the first rays of the morning sun.

# Chapter Fourteen

The night after she found Max Swinton's statue, Heckie couldn't sleep. She kept thinking how wicked Dora Mayberry had been, snatching the politician from her and doing poor Mr Knacksap out of his tiger. Copying Heckie's hat had been bad enough, but this was far, far worse.

But the more she tried to tell herself how awful Dora had been, the more she kept remembering things from the thirty years that both of them had been at school. The time that Dora had cut her toenails for her because Heckie had hurt her back during chimney landing practice. The way Dora always picked the earwigs out of the Hoover bag when it was her turn to clean the dorm because she knew how it upset Heckie when earwigs were put in the bin. And what a netball player the witch had been!

Was it possible that Dora hadn't meant to upset Heckie? Did she too just think that Max Swinton ought not to be around any longer? And where was Dora? Could she have moved to Wellbridge?

In the morning, as soon as she had fed the animals in the shop and given the dragworm his princess, Heckie went to see Mr Gurgle to ask him if he'd heard anything about the stone witch. The cheese wizard was in a bad mood because his Stilton had developed a limp, but he tried to be helpful.

'I haven't heard anything myself,' he said, 'but Frieda Fennel did say as how a stone-mason's business out in Fetlington has changed hands – that's past the prison, you know. She did say that the quality of work was very high and she was wondering.'

So Heckie went to see the garden witch who was wheeling a single artichoke along in her wheelbarrow, her muscles straining because it was the size of an armchair, and she said, yes, she was almost sure the new owner of the stone-mason's was a witch. There was something about the garden gnomes that was special.

But when Heckie had got the address, she couldn't make up her mind. Suppose Dora was still angry with her? Also, there'd been rather a fuss about Max Swinton since statues, unlike animals, can't run away or be sent to the zoo. Questions were being asked and though no one guessed the truth, there was a lot of puzzlement.

She was still deciding what to do when she met Mr Knacksap for tea at The Copper Kettle.

The furrier had gone off in a rage when he heard that he wasn't getting his tiger, but since then he had done some serious thinking. A witch who could turn people into animals and another witch who could turn people into stone . . . What did that suggest? To Mr Knacksap it suggested riches beyond his dreams, a life of plenty in which he need never work again. The plan he now came up with could only have been

95

worked out by someone half mad with cruelty and greed, but Mr Knacksap was exactly such a man.

So he wrote a little note to Heckie saying he was sorry he had lost his temper, but he'd been so upset at disappointing his friend who was a lord, and inviting Heckie to meet him for tea.

Heckie was terribly pleased to see him and she asked him at once what he thought she should do about Dora Mayberry. 'You see, I do hate to go on quarrelling, but I couldn't bear it if she was unkind to me. What do you think I should do, Li-Li?'

This gave Mr Knacksap just the opening he was looking for. 'I tell you what, my dear,' he said, smiling his gooey smile, 'since you're such a shy and delicate little thing, why don't you let me go? I'll give her your message and tell her you want to be friends and see what she says.'

'Oh, would you, Li-Li? That's so kind of you. So like you. I'll write her a letter and give it to you.'

So Heckie wrote a letter in which she said that while she had been rather cross about Mr Swinton, who was really hers, if Dora really hadn't known what Heckie was going to do, then she was happy to let bygones be bygones. 'Because I have missed you very much, dear Dora,' wrote Heckie, and then she sealed the envelope and gave it to Mr Knacksap to take to her friend.

But what did Mr Knacksap do?

As soon as he was out of sight, he tore the letter into little pieces and threw them away. Not even into a bin because he was a litter lout as well as a creep – just away in the street where the wind blew them all over the place. Then he hailed a taxi and drove to the stone-mason's yard.

Dora Mayberry was in her overalls and Wellington boots, chipping with a chisel at the nose of a Greek hero whom a rich businessman wanted to put in his park. Just as Heckie kept an ordinary pet shop to earn her living in which the rabbits and guinea pigs really were rabbits and guinea pigs and not changed people, so Dora did ordinary stonework for anyone who would pay her and she did it very well. The hero was the kind with a lion skin round his shoulder and a lot of muscles and a club, and Mr Knacksap stood for a while watching before he coughed softly and asked if he was in the presence of Miss Dora Mayberry.

'That's me,' said Dora, nodding, and she wiped her chisel and looked at the handsome man in his dark coat with the raccoon collar and the black hat. 'Come in,' she said, blushing a little because there had been no gentlemen in the Witch Academy and she was very shy.

Mr Knacksap followed her in, his nose twitching with curiosity. So this homely woman could turn a man into stone. Quite a lot of men if need be!

'I've come with a message from a friend of yours. A Miss Hecate Tenbury-Smith.'

'Heckie!' Dora's round little eyes lit up. 'How is she? Tell me about her, please. Oh, I have missed her so!'

For it was true, Dora had not meant to annoy Heckie. Though she had moved back to Wellbridge, hoping to make it up with her friend, she had not dared to go and see her. Suppose Heckie snubbed her? Then she had read about Max Swinton in the paper and become very upset. A man like that shouldn't be allowed to exist, she thought, and when Swinton took a stroll in the park, she'd been ready for him. It had been hard work dragging him to the right spot, mounting him properly, but she'd done it and been proud of her handiwork. In the old days she'd have gone straight to Heckie and shown her what she'd done.

So now she waited eagerly for what Mr Knacksap had to say.

'I'm afraid your friend is absolutely furious with you. In fact you can hardly call Miss Tenbury-Smith your friend. She never wants to see you again.'

'Oh, oh!' Poor Dora put her hand to her mouth and her eyes widened in sorrow and dismay. 'But why? Why?'

'She's very angry with you about Mr Swinton's statue. She was going to change him into a tiger and everything was prepared. But it isn't just that. She feels very bitter about the hat and everything. She sent me to tell you that she never wants to set eyes on you again.'

Poor Dora! She was a solid, well-built woman, but she just seemed to shrink as Mr Knacksap spoke. He went on telling lies for another ten minutes and then he went back to Heckie.

Heckie was waiting for him, her pop eyes bright with hope.

'I'm afraid it's no good, dear,' he said. 'Dora Mayberry never wants to see you again as long as she lives. I won't repeat some of the things she said about you, but they were quite terrible.'

98

Heckie turned pale with disappointment. She had come down to meet the furrier in the street because the dragworm was at home, and now she leant against a lamp-post, almost as though she might faint.

'Don't be sad, my little prettikins,' said Mr Knacksap, taking her hand. 'Your Li-Li will look after you.'

The horrible man's plan was clear now in his head. He'd been excited at the idea of having one tiger skin to sell, but this . . . If he pulled it off, he'd be the richest furrier in the world!

And he would pull it off. He had one witch in his power. Now he would get the other one too.

And then . . .!

# Chapter Fifteen

Mr Knacksap now began to court Heckie seriously. He came to see her on Tuesdays and Thursdays and Saturdays, and on those days Daniel came at tea time to take the dragworm for a walk. He brought her red roses which he stole from the garden of the blind lady, and plain chocolates with hard centres because they were her favourites.

And one afternoon, sitting on the sofa in her cosy flat, he told her that he wanted to change his life.

'I'm tired of living in town among the fumes and the dust,' said Mr Knacksap. 'I want to go and live in the country where the air is clear. In the Lake District, where there are mountains and heather and . . . er . . . lakes. I want to milk cows!' said Mr Knacksap, waving his hand.

'Sheep, dear,' said Heckie. 'It's sheep you have in hill country.'

Mr Knacksap frowned. He did not like to be interrupted and was not quite sure if he wanted to milk sheep.

'Chickens too!' he cried. 'I want to get up at daybreak and look for brown eggs in the straw!'

He fished in the pocket of his jacket and showed Heckie a picture. It was of a pretty whitewashed cottage with a porch, standing in the shelter of a high hill. A stream ran through the garden, with alder trees along its banks, and a dovecote covered in honeysuckle stood by the gate.

'Oh, Li-Li, what a pretty place!'

'It's called Paradise Cottage,' said Mr Knacksap. 'And what I want more than anything in the world is to live there.'

Heckie was silent. When you love somebody it is sad to think that they may go and live a long way away, but she tried to be brave. 'If that's what you want, you must do it, Li-Li. But, oh, I shall miss you.'

Mr Knacksap seized Heckie's hand. 'No, no, dearest Hecate – you don't understand! I want you to come with me. I want us to live there together! I am asking you to marry me!'

In the staffroom of Wellbridge Junior School, they were once again talking about Daniel Trent.

'He's looking thoroughly peaky again,' said the deputy head. 'Just when he seemed so much brighter. I wonder if I ought to have a word with those professors?'

But it wasn't the fault of Daniel's parents that he was unhappy. They did what they had always done. It was Heckie's engagement that had made Daniel so wretched. If she'd just been going to marry Mr Knacksap, it would have been bad enough, but she was going to live miles and miles away in the Lake District. And so soon! Mr Knacksap wanted to have the wedding before the end of the month.

'You'll come and stay with us often and often,' Heckie kept saying, and Daniel always answered: 'Yes, of course I will.' But he knew that he wouldn't.

Mr Knacksap didn't like children; anyone could see that.

'I suppose Heckie must be very happy,' said Sumi when the children met at break. 'But she looks awfully tired.'

'She's worried about the dragworm,' said Daniel. 'She can't take him with her because of Mr Knacksap being allergous or whatever he is.'

'Well, I think he's up to something,' said Joe. He was sitting on the coal-bunker eating a banana and looking more like a small ape than ever. 'I believe he's marrying her for a reason. And why can't he ever come and see her on a Monday or a Wednesday or a Friday? What's he doing the other days, do you suppose? I tell you, he's a crook; I just know it.'

But what could the children do?

'If we try and warn her, she'll never believe us,' said Sumi.

'No,' said Daniel thoughtfully. 'She wouldn't believe *us*. But there's someone she'd *have* to believe, isn't there?'

The others looked at him. 'Yes,' said Joe slowly. 'I see what you mean.'

Mr Knacksap opened the door of his shop and stepped into the street. He was carrying a bunch of roses and a box of chocolates, but the roses were white, not red, and the chocolates were not plain ones with hard centres, but milky ones with soft centres.

There were other differences too. When he went to see Heckie, the furrier always wore a dark suit and had his hair parted in the middle. Now he was wearing a white suit and his hair was parted at the side. What was the same, though, was the greedy, furtive look on his face.

He crossed Market Square and made his way down the narrow road which led to the bus station. A Number 33 was waiting to set off for Fetlington, on the north side of the town, and as he rode past the prison and the football ground, the furrier closed his eyes and gloated. In a month he'd be safely in Spain, leading a life of luxury. Fast cars, casinos, beautiful girls to massage his feet and scoop the wax out of his ears as he lay beside the swimming pool!

At Fetlington Green, he got off and walked past a row of shops, then turned down the hill towards a piece of open ground with a barn and workshops. The sound of chipping and hammering came to him across the still air and he smiled his oily smile. She was a real worker, you had to give her that!

'Coo-ee,' called Mr Knacksap, as he opened the gates of the stone-mason's yard. 'It's me!'

The chipping stopped. Dora Mayberry came out of the shed, wiping her hands. 'Lewis!' she said, smiling happily, and bent to sniff the roses. 'Your tea's all ready. I've got those cup cakes you like so much. Come on in and make yourself comfortable.'

When Dora had heard that Heckie was still cross with her, she'd gone to pieces. She fed her hat with any old rubbish and she didn't care what she turned to stone – not just the fish fingers and her potted geranium and the bobble on her bedroom slippers, but the ointment she was supposed to rub on her chest for her cough, so that life in the cottage became quite impossible. Even the ghost in the wardrobe got harder and began to creak like a rusty hinge. It's pretty certain that someone would have come and taken Dora away to a mental hospital before much longer, but one Wednesday afternoon there was a knock at the door and a visitor stood there, carrying a bunch of flowers and a box of chocolates.

After which a new life began for Dora Mayberry. Twice a week, on Wednesdays and Fridays, the tall, dark man who had brought the message from Heckie came to tea. She didn't like to ask him too many questions, but she learnt that he was called Lewis Kingman (she had already noticed the initials L.K. stamped on his wallet) and that he worked in insurance. But he wasn't happy in his work and now, biting into a chocolate cup cake, he told her what he wanted to do with his life.

'You see, dearest Dora, I feel I cannot go on living in town,' he said. 'My lungs are delicate. I need to be in the country. Somewhere open and clean. In a house like this.' And from the pocket of his suit he brought out a picture.

'What a pretty place!' said Dora. 'The dovecote and the trees, and the way the river runs through the garden!'

'It's called Paradise Cottage,' said Mr Knacksap. 'And what I want more than anything else in the world, is to live there with you!'

For a moment he wondered whether to go down on his knees, but Dora wasn't very good at dusting, and anyway there was no need – the silly witch was looking adoringly into his eyes.

'Oh, Lewis!' she said. 'You mean you want to marry me?'

'I do,' said Mr Knacksap.

The next day, he bought two of the cheapest engagement rings he could find and had them engraved with his initials. But it wasn't of the two bamboozled witches that he was thinking as he left the shop. It was of a man in a distant country who was almost as crazy and greedy as he was himself.

# Chapter Sixteen

The name of this man was Abdul el Hammed and he was an exceedingly rich sheikh who lived between the Zagros Mountains and the Caspian Sea. The sheikh was rich because his country was full of oil wells, but he was also very old-fashioned – so old-fashioned that he had one hundred and fifty wives, just as Eastern rulers used to do in the olden days. The wives lived in a palace all of their own and the sheikh liked to show them off, all dressed alike in beautiful clothes and fabulous jewellery, so that everyone would be amazed that anyone could have so many women and be so generous.

In the summer, the country in which the sheikh lived was very hot, but in the winter, because there were high mountains near by, it was very cold – and it was then that he liked to dress his one hundred and fifty wives in valuable fur coats. But it is not easy to find a hundred and fifty coats made of price-less skins and all alike. The sheikh had been looking round and had sent messengers to all the furriers in Europe and he had not found what he was looking for.

This sheikh wanted to see every one of his wives dressed in a coat made of snow leopards.

Tigers are beautiful and exciting, so are jaguars and ocelots, and people who like fur coats swear by sable or mink. But in all the world, there is nothing like a coat made of snow leopards.

Snow leopards live in the highest mountains in the world – on the slopes of the Himalayas and the Karakoram, where there are no people, only ice and eagles and the sighing of the wind. They are so graceful and so fearless – and above all so rare – that to look at one is to feel a lump come into your throat. There are so few left now that to shoot or trap one is to risk being sent to prison and only a person with no soul would dream of trying it. To kill one snow leopard and make his skin into a fur coat would be almost impossible. To find three hundred (because at least two leopards are needed for a single coat) . . . well, no one but a mad, rich sheikh would even dream of it.

But the sheikh Abdul el Hammed did dream of it. The more he couldn't have what he wanted, the more he was determined to have it. He had offered a thousand pounds for a snow leopard skin and then fifteen hundred, and at last two thousand and more just for one skin. But there simply weren't any snow leopards to be had. Not even the greediest people were willing to break the law which protected these marvellous and unusual beasts.

And then came the day when Mr Flitchbody, a skin trader who operated in London, but had a network of trappers and hunters all over the world, got a telephone call.

'Hello. Is that you, Flitchbody?' a throaty voice said.

'Yes, Flitchbody speaking. Who is that?'

'It's Knacksap here. Lionel Knacksap from

Wellbridge. Tell me, is that sheikh of yours still after snow leopard pelts?'

'You bet he is. Three hundred, he wants, and he'll sell his soul to get them – and I can't find one.'

'Well, I can,' said Mr Knacksap. 'I can get him the full quantity. If the price is right.'

'The price is two thousand eight hundred per skin and I take ten per cent. But I don't believe you for a moment.'

'Well, you'd better believe me. I've found someone who's been breeding them in secret. I can send you the bodies, but you'll have to get them skinned down in London and no questions asked. Can you fix that?'

'I can fix it. But I still think you're bluffing.'

'Well, I'm not. I'll want the money in cash. Three-quarters of a million in notes, can you do that?'

'If you can get me three hundred snow leopards, there's nothing I can't do.'

'I'll keep you posted,' said Mr Knacksap, and put down the phone.

# Chapter Seventeen

Mr Knacksap and Heckie were sitting side by side on Heckie's sofa and being romantic. Mr Knacksap was holding Heckie's hand – the one that didn't have the Knuckle of Power – and they were looking into the gas fire and dreaming dreams.

Or rather, Mr Knacksap was dreaming dreams. Heckie's foot had gone to sleep which sometimes happens when you are being romantic, but she didn't like to say so.

'I was thinking, my dear,' said Mr Knacksap, 'about when we are married and living in our cottage in the hills. Paradise Cottage.'

'Yes, dear?' said Heckie. 'What were you thinking about it?'

'I was thinking how beautiful the mountains are up there. Beautiful, but bare. Terribly bare.'

'Well, yes. Of course there is the heather, isn't there?' said Heckie. 'That's very pretty when it flowers.'

'But it only flowers in August. I would like to be able to look up at the hills and see them covered with something really wonderful. With animals that are happy in high places and that are graceful and lovely and a joy to gaze at all the year round. Heather is all right for ladies,' said Mr Knacksap, 'but gentlemen like something a little stronger.'

'What sort of something?' Heckie wanted to know.

Mr Knacksap let go of her hand and turned to look into her eyes. 'I am going to tell you a secret, Hecate,' he said. 'Something I've not told anyone in my life. Always, I've had the same dream. That I wake in the morning and I look up – and there, on the mountain-side above me, are the loveliest and most impressive animals in the world.'

Heckie was very interested. 'Really, dear? And what are they?'

Mr Knacksap blew his nose. Then he said: 'Snow leopards.'

'Snow leopards?' Heckie was very surprised. 'But, dearest, you don't find snow leopards in the Lake District. They're not English things at all. You find them in the Himalayas.'

'I know, dearest,' said Mr Knacksap. 'So far you don't find them in England. But you *could*.' He seized both her hands. 'You could make my dream come true,' he said, rolling his eyes. 'You, my dearest, sweetest witch, could fill the hillside with snow leopards. You could grant me my greatest wish! Every morning I would lift up my eyes and there they would be! They're the most valuable . . . I mean, the most beautiful creatures in the world. Their pelts . . . I mean, their fur, is the deepest, the palest; their tails are thick and long. They have golden eyes and every day as I ate my porridge and kippers, which you would cook for me, I would see them roaming free and lovely over the hills. If I could do that, I think I would be the happiest man in the world.'

110

He looked sideways under his sinister eyebrows at Heckie who was looking very worried indeed.

'But, dearest, a whole hillside of snow leopards . . . I don't see how I could do that. And I'm afraid they'd eat the sheep.'

'Oh, but once the snow leopards came, it would become an animal reserve, that's certain. And think of the tourist trade, and the work it would bring to the unemployed.'

'I could make one or two leopards for you; I'm sure to meet one or two really wicked people before we get married. But a whole hillside – I don't see how I could possibly do that. How many do you want?'

'Three hundred!' said Mr Knacksap firmly. 'At least.'

Heckie leapt to her feet. 'Three hundred! My dearest Li-Li, that's quite impossible. There probably aren't three hundred wicked people in Britain, let alone Wellbridge!'

'Yes, there are, my treasure. There are three hundred wicked people right here in this town. Very wicked people. Murderers and terrorists and embezzlers and thugs. People who shouldn't be eating their heads off at the government's expense. People who'd be much happier roaming the hills as free and graceful leopards for me to look at when I ate my kippers.'

'But where?' asked Heckie. 'What do you mean?'

'In the prison, of course. In Wellbridge prison not a mile from here.'

He leant back, well pleased with himself, and waited for Heckie to tell him how clever he was.

111

'You mean you want me to turn all the prisoners into leopards?' asked Heckie, looking stunned.

'I do,' said the furrier smugly.

The witch shook her head. 'I'm sorry, Li-Li, but I can't do that.'

Mr Knacksap was absolutely furious. How *dare* she go against his wishes? 'Can't! What do you mean, you can't?' he said, and turned away so that she wouldn't see him grinding his teeth.

Heckie sighed. 'You see, people get sent to prison for all sorts of things. There's no way I could be sure that all of them are wicked. If someone had bopped his mother-in-law with a meat cleaver, he mightn't be really bad. It would depend—'

'Everybody in Wellbridge jail is bad,' hissed the furrier. 'It's a high security prison. That means that anyone who gets out will certainly strike again. And anyway, I'd have thought you'd want to make your Li-Li happy. I'd have thought—'

'I do want to make you happy,' said Heckie. 'I want to *terribly*. But one has to do what is *right* and changing people who are not wicked is Not Right.'

It was at this moment that the doorbell rang and Daniel and Joe came in, carefully carrying a large, round box covered in brown paper.

'We took this from the delivery boy,' said Joe. 'It's addressed to both of you. I expect it's a wedding present.'

He handed the box to the furrier who took it and simpered. If people were sending silver or valuable glass, he'd have to be sure of getting it to his place so that he could sell it before he bolted for Spain.

'But where's the dragworm?' asked Heckie,

looking at Daniel. 'I thought you were taking him out.'

'I was,' said Daniel. 'But I met Sumi and she wanted to take him for a bit.'

Heckie nodded and smiled at Mr Knacksap who was eagerly undoing the parcel. Perhaps it was a soup tureen, thought the furrier – that could fetch a couple of hundred. Or an antique clock . . . But as he tore off the wrappings, his look of greed turned to one of puzzlement. For there seemed to be holes in the cardboard box and surely neither soup tureens nor clocks needed to breathe?

'Ugh! It's a monster! A horrible diseased THING full of boils. Get rid of it! Get it out! Shoo!'

The boys stood very still and looked at Heckie. Now at last she would see! It had been very hard to bring Heckie's familiar into the room, knowing what would happen to him, but the children would have done anything to save the witch.

'It's the dragworm, Heckie,' said Daniel quietly.

Too late, Mr Knacksap realized his mistake. He began to cough and splutter and totter round the room. 'Oh, help! My asthma! I'm choking! I can't breathe!'

But for once, Heckie didn't rush to the furrier's side. She had gathered up the dragworm, so shocked by what she saw that at first she couldn't speak.

Her familiar had been in a bad way when he was close to Mrs Winneypeg, but it was nothing to the state he was in now. The hair on his topknot wasn't just white, it was as brittle as that of a ninety-year-old. Some of his scales had actually flaked off, his eyes were filmed over. As for his other end – the most

113

hardened sick nurse would have shed tears when she saw the dragworm's tail.

'Oh, you poor, poor love; you poor thing!' cried Heckie – and as she stroked his head, there came from his throat that ghostly, faint, heartbreaking: 'Quack!'

'I don't understand it,' said Heckie. 'What has happened? What made him come on like that?'

It was Joe who spoke. 'He did. Mr Knacksap did. That's why we brought the dragworm, so that you could see what kind of a person—'

'Stop it! That's enough!' Heckie's pop eyes snapped with temper. 'How *dare* you speak like that about the man I'm going to marry?'

But she looked at Mr Knacksap in a very puzzled way.

The furrier, though, had recovered himself. Still pretending to cough and wheeze, he drew himself up to his full height and pointed at the boys.

'You lying, evil children! How dare you tell poor Heckie such untruths? As though I didn't see you. I saw you quite distinctly taking this poor, sensitive creature right up to the prison gate and along the prison walls. Quite distinctly, I saw you, and I thought then how foolish it was to risk him like that.'

'We didn't!' said Daniel and Joe together. 'Honestly we didn't! We wouldn't do a silly thing like that.'

'In the tartan shopping basket,' Mr Knacksap went on. 'I saw you not half an hour ago.' He turned to Heckie. 'Now will you believe me? Now will you

114

believe me when I tell you how evil those prisoners are?'

Heckie looked desperately from the furrier to the boys and back again. She was a sensible witch, but no one can be in love and stay sensible for long.

'Oh, Daniel . . . Joe . . . that was foolish of you. Run along now and I'll put him in the bath. He'll soon be better.'

So the children left, wretched and defeated, having made the dragworm ill for nothing. And that night, Heckie phoned the furrier.

'All right, Lionel,' she said wearily. 'I'll do what you ask. You shall have your leopards.'

To the stone witch, Mr Knacksap didn't say anything about snow leopards. What he spoke to Dora about was his Cousin Alfred.

'What's happened to my poor dear cousin is the one thing that is spoiling my happiness,' he said, dabbing his eyes with his handkerchief.

'What has happened to him?' asked Dora Mayberry.

'He is in prison,' said Mr Knacksap, and sighed. 'Here in Wellbridge. That sweet, sensitive soul eating his heart out among all those ruffians.'

'Oh, Lewis, that's so sad. How did it happen?'

'It wasn't Alfred's fault, I promise you. He was led astray by bad people. If only you could have seen him as a little boy. We were such friends. He used to build sandcastles for me, and whenever his mummy bought him a lollipop, he would let me have a lick. Look at his photograph – isn't that an innocent face?'

Dora took the picture and said, yes it was, and fancy him having ringlets! (The picture was actually of a child actor who had played Little Lord Fauntleroy in a film.)

'What is he in prison for?' she asked.

'He stole the purse out of an old lady's handbag. The wicked people he fell in with made him do it.' He dabbed at his eyes again and sniffed. 'If only I could get him out of prison, I would send him to a wonderful mind doctor that I know of. Then he'd soon be well again and never do anything bad any more.'

'But how could you, Lewis? How could you get him out?'

This time, Mr Knacksap did go down on his knees. After all, soon he would be able to buy dozens of pairs of new trousers, hundreds of them . . .

'With you to help me, dearest Dora, I could do it. If you could turn the prison guards to stone, just for one night, I could get him out.'

Dora thought for a while and then she said that if it was only his Cousin Alfred he was going to get out, and if she could turn the guards back into people the next day, she didn't mind. 'I couldn't leave them stone, of course, because they aren't wicked. Not so far as I know. But for a night it shouldn't hurt.'

'Oh, my dearest, dearest Dora,' said Mr Knacksap, 'you've made me so happy! I just couldn't face sitting over my porridge and kippers in Paradise Cottage, knowing that poor dear Alfred was lying in a cold stone cell.'

Then he went back to town and put up a big

116

FOR SALE notice outside his shop. Everything was ready – and there was nothing between him and three-quarters of a million pounds.

# Chapter Eighteen

Mr Knacksap's plan was simple. He would take Dora to the prison as soon as it was dark and when she'd turned the guards to stone, he'd send her packing. Then two of his accomplices, Nat and Billy, would drive the vans into the prison – they were huge ones, hired from a circus, and would take the leopards comfortably enough. Nat knew about electronics too; there'd be no trouble with the alarm system with him around.

When they'd taken over the prison, he'd go and fetch Heckie and let her in by a side door so that she wouldn't see the stone guards, and bring the prisoners to her one by one – and when she'd changed them into leopards, she'd be sent packing too.

And then the following morning both witches would meet on the station platform to catch the 10.55 to the Lake District! It was this part of the plan that always made Mr Knacksap titter out loud when he thought of it. For he had told both witches to wait for him at the Windermere Hotel. He had told both of them that he would marry them in a little grey church by the edge of the water. Both of them thought they were going to live happily ever after with him in Paradise Cottage!

If only he could have been there to see them

scratch each other's eyes out! But by that time the leopards would be dead and skinned, and he'd be on the way to Spain!

As for how to kill three hundred leopards without marking their pelts, Mr Knacksap had got that sorted out too. About five miles to the east of Wellbridge, there was a derelict stately home called Hankley Hall. No one went there – it was said to be haunted – but some of the rooms were still in good repair. The ballroom, in particular, had windows that fitted well and a wooden gallery that ran round the top. The man he'd hired to do the actual killing said it was a doddle. You just lobbed a canister down from the gallery and waited.

When you wanted to kill someone and leave no mark, Sid had said, there was nothing like plain, old-fashioned gas.

Farewell parties are often sad, and Heckie's was sadder than most.

She gave it on her last day before leaving Wellbridge, and she gave it in the afternoon because in the evening she had to go and change the prisoners. Heckie had told no one of Mr Knacksap's plan – not even her helpers – but they could see that she looked tired and strained, and not really like a bride.

The furrier couldn't be at the party, but almost all her friends were there and had brought presents. Sumi's parents had sent a huge tin of biscuits with a picture of Buckingham Palace on the lid, Joe had made some book-ends, and the cheese wizard brought a round Dutch cheese.

119

'It can't do much,' he explained. 'Just a few centimetres. But if you're going to eat it, it won't matter.'

Madame Rosalia gave her a make-up bag full of useful things: pimples, blotches, pockmarks and a tuft of hair for joining her eyebrows together; and the garden witch brought a cauliflower which got stuck in the door and had to be cut free with a hatchet.

But the best present – really an amazing present – came from Boris Chomsky, and it was nothing less than a hot air balloon which really did fly on the hot air talked by politicians!

Boris had been very upset by what happened at the Tritlington Poultry Unit and he began to work much harder at his invention. He got out all his books of spells and studied late into the night. Then he went up to the Houses of Parliament with his tape recorder hidden under his greatcoat and started to record the speeches that the members made. He took down the waffle that the Minister for Health talked about it being people's own fault if they got ill, and the piffle that the Minister for Employment talked about there really being lots of lovely jobs for everyone if only they weren't too lazy to look, and the garbage that the MPs shouted at each other during Question Time.

Then he went back to his garage and boiled things in crucibles and burnt them in thuribles – and at last the day came when he put a tape of the Chancellor's speech at the Lord Mayor's Banquet into one of the fuel converters, and the balloon rose up so quickly that it hit the roof.

So now they all trooped across the road and round

the corner to Boris's garage and admired Heckie's balloon (which was grey because it rains a lot in the Lake District) and the other balloons which he had converted so that they could be used by any wizard or witch who wanted them.

But when Heckie had thanked him again and again, and taken her guests back to the party, her face grew very sad and her eyes went more and more often to the door to look for the one person who hadn't come.

'I'm sure he'll be along soon,' said Sumi, who always seemed to know what was troubling people. 'I expect the professors have made him do some extra piano practice.'

But the clock struck five, and then six, and Heckie had to face the fact that the boy she loved as though he was her son had not even troubled to say goodbye.

# Chapter Nineteen

The prison crouched on its hill, surrounded by warehouses and factories. Even by day it was a grim building, but at night, rearing out of the mist, it looked deeply sinister.

Dora and Mr Knacksap walked up to the main gate just as the clock was striking eleven. There was no one about; they could hear the echo of their own footsteps. Dora wasn't so much nervous as shy, and she was carrying a powerful electric torch because stone magic depends on being able to see the victim's eyes.

'I'm sure you're going to do splendidly, dear,' said Mr Knacksap in his oily voice – and pressed the big brass bell.

They could hear it shrilling and then a uniformed guard came out, carrying a gun.

'My friend is feeling faint,' said Mr Knacksap. 'I wonder if you could help?'

'This isn't a bloomin' hospital,' said the guard. 'It's a pris—'

And then he didn't say anything more.

It was almost too easy. If Mr Knacksap hadn't been so ignorant, he'd have realized how honoured he was to see such a powerful witch at work. A second guard appeared, wanting to know what was going on, and then he too fell silent. Mr Knacksap pushed Dora through the crack in the gate and into the guardroom where two more men were playing cards – and in an instant even the playing cards they were holding turned to stone.

Within half an hour, the prison was full of statues. Statues of the warders in charge of each corridor, one caught as he peered into the spy-hole of a cell . . . A statue of the chief warder, sitting in his office – a statue with ear-phones because he'd been listening to the radio to make the long night pass more quickly. There was a statue of a patrol man, still shouting at his dog, and a most graceful one of the dog itself, an Alsatian whom Dora had looked at just before it sprang at her throat.

'Well, that seems to be it,' said Mr Knacksap when they had walked up and down the corridors and the winding iron stairs without anybody challenging them. 'Now you just go home and make sure you're on that train, otherwise you won't be ready for your Lewis when he comes.'

Dora had hoped he might ask her to stay till he had found his Cousin Alfred. She was curious to see what a little boy with ringlets, who'd let Lewis have a lick of his lollipop, looked like after his time in prison. But the furrier took her firmly to the gate. He didn't even say thank you, or hail a taxi, or give her a kiss.

But Dora was a humble witch. She turned up her collar and trudged out into the night.

'Oh, Li-Li, not that one! Please! He looks so young.'

An hour had passed and Heckie sat in a small cloakroom off the prison yard, facing her first prisoner. She had kicked off her shoe and her Toe of Transformation felt icy on the bare tiles.

'Surely he can't have done anything terrible?' Heckie went on.

The furrier leant forward. 'He strangled a little girl in cold blood,' he hissed – and the prisoner looked up, puzzled. They couldn't be talking about him, surely? He was doing three years for housebreaking.

But Heckie had believed Mr Knacksap. She leant forward and touched the young man with her knuckle – and then even the horrible Mr Knacksap gasped in wonder.

There are no words that can describe the beauty of a snow leopard. Their coats are a misty grey with black rosettes that are clouded by the depth of the rich fur. Their golden eyes stare out of a face that belongs on shields or banners, it is so grave and mythical – and when they move, their long, thick tails curve and coil and circle in a never-ending dance.

Mr Knacksap had retreated behind a chair, his hand in the pocket of his coat where he kept a gun, but Heckie knew her job. She had made the leopard as sleepy as the prisoner had been. The great cat yawned slowly and delicately. Then it loped off, out of the door, through the wire tunnel, and up the ramp to the first lorry which had SIMPSON'S CIRCUS painted on its side.

Everything was going the way Mr Knacksap had planned. The prisoners had been woken and told they were going to be moved to a new jail with better food and more space, and they shuffled out of their cells, half-asleep, giving no trouble. Nat, who brought them to Heckie, didn't need the sub-machine gun he'd insisted on carrying.

And how Heckie worked! She turned one prisoner and then two and three and four . . . Sometimes she stopped when a particularly innocent-looking prisoner was brought to her, but always Mr Knacksap would bend over her and hiss some frightful lie into her ear and she would go on with her job.

When she had changed over fifty prisoners, she swayed and her head fell forward. Mr Knacksap had no idea what he was asking her to do. Turning one person into an animal can leave a witch completely exhausted. Turning three hundred . . . well, witches have died from over-straining themselves like that. But the furrier knew exactly how to get round her.

'Dearest Hecate,' he said with his gooey smile, 'if you knew how happy you are making me!'

That did it, of course. Heckie lifted her head, blew on her throbbing knuckle and got to work again. And by one in the morning, her task was done.

But if Heckie had hoped that Mr Knacksap would thank her or give her a kiss or order a taxi, she, like Dora, had hoped in vain. As the door of the lorry slammed on the last of the leopards, Heckie let herself out of a side door and half limped, half staggered, home.

But though she fell straight into bed, Heckie couldn't sleep. Her Toe of Transformation ached and stabbed every time she moved, and when her knuckle caught on the sheet, she flinched with pain.

After an hour, she got up and fetched the dragworm and packed him carefully in his tartan shopping basket. What she had decided to do probably wouldn't work out, but it was her only chance, for familiars never thrive except with witches, and powerful ones at that. It wasn't as though she was asking anything for herself. Heckie knew that Dora wanted nothing more to do with *her* – but could anybody turn away something so appealing and unusual as the dragworm?

Dora, too, was overtired and couldn't sleep, and after a while she gave up trying and put on her boiler suit and went downstairs.

The wardrobe was lying flat in the van that Dora had hired to take her furniture to be stored. Everything else had already gone to the warehouse to wait till Dora knew what she would need in Paradise Cottage. Only the wardrobe was left and as Dora approached, the wood spirit floated out and gave her a shy and wavery smile.

Dora had not wanted a ghost at all, and when the spirit first started floating about among her coathangers, she had been quite annoyed. But gradually she had become fond of it. It still didn't say much except 'Don't chop down the wardrobe,' but in its own way the thing was affectionate. Dora would have liked to take the wardrobe with her to Paradise Cottage, but Lewis did not care for ghosts. The first time he had come to tea and the spirit had called down from the bedroom, Lewis had leapt from the sofa and dropped his cup cake on the floor.

Dora had found some people to buy the stonemason's business, but suppose they got annoyed with the poor spirit? Suppose in a fit of anger they *did* chop down the wardrobe. Dora would never forgive herself.

Could her friend really refuse to take in this doleful ghost? It wasn't as though Dora was asking anything for herself. She knew Heckie never wanted to see *her* again. But could Heckie, who had never turned away a stray in her life, refuse to give a home to this poor sad thing?

And Dora climbed into the cab and drove up the hill towards the town.

# Chapter Twenty

The cheese wizard went to bed early. Serving in his shop by day and doing magic on his cheeses at night made Mr Gurgle very tired. But on the night of Heckie's farewell party, he was woken in the small hours by an odd tapping noise. Tap, tap, tap, it went, and then stopped again, and just as he was dropping off, it began once more.

'Oh, bother!' said Mr Gurgle, and got out of bed and put on his slippers. The tapping seemed to be coming from right below him, from the cellar. Could his prize cheese be learning to tap dance? Sometimes people who couldn't walk very well got on better when they tried to move to music.

But when he got down to the cellar, the Stilton lay quietly on its shelf, looking as fast asleep as only a cheese can do.

The wizard scratched his head. Had he imagined the tapping? No, there it was again. Sounding louder, sounding really frantic. But it wasn't in his cellar, it was in the cellar next door. Which was very strange ... Because the shop next door belonged to the furrier, Mr Knacksap, who had gone away to get ready for his wedding to Heckie. Mr Knacksap's shop should have been empty.

Another burst of tapping ... Mr Gurgle went up to the dividing wall and tapped in turn, and the tapping became louder. Something or someone was trapped in there. The wizard slipped on his coat and went outside. The front of the furrier's shop was locked – the back too. But there was a grating across the top of the cellar steps, out in the back yard. He fetched a stepladder and climbed over the wall, wobbling a little, for he was holding a torch in one hand.

The grating was ancient and rusty, but though Mr Gurgle was weedy, he was also obstinate. He tugged and he tugged and at last it came away and he could make his way carefully down the cellar steps.

At the bottom, curled in a heap, lay a boy. Blood had hardened on his forehead and his face; there was more blood on his hands where he had pounded the rough stone wall.

It was only when he tried to speak, muttering words that made no sense at all, that the wizard recognized Daniel.

Everyone had been worried about Heckie's engagement to the furrier, but as the day of the wedding grew closer, Daniel became quite frantic. Though he knew that Heckie was a powerful witch, he couldn't rid himself of the feeling that some frightful harm would come to her through Mr Knacksap.

He had bought Heckie a present: a tea-making machine which dropped exactly the right number of bags into the pot. He was actually wrapping it up when he decided not to go to the party. Instead, he made his way to the furrier's shop in Market Square. Perhaps even now he could still get proof of the furrier's treachery.

Over the FOR SALE notice, another notice had been plastered, saying SOLD. The beaver cape had been taken from the window. But, to Daniel's surprise, the door of the shop was ajar. Mr Knacksap's cleaning lady, in a very nasty temper, was just leaving.

'If you want him, you'd better come in and wait,' she said. 'I'm not hanging around any longer. If he doesn't want to give me a bit of a farewell tip like any decent gentleman would, then good riddance to him.'

She left, and Daniel slipped in to the furrier's office. It was stripped and bare. Beside the desk stood three leather suitcases with gaudy labels.

L. KNACKSAP, HOTEL SPLENDISSIMA, ALICANTE, SPAIN, read Daniel.

*Spain?* Why Spain? thought Daniel. Surely it was beside Lake Windermere that the furrier was going to marry Heckie?

At that moment he heard the sound of a key turning in the lock. Mr Knacksap coming back for his luggage! There was a cupboard in the corner for coats and overalls. Daniel slipped inside, his heart pounding, and closed the door.

Mr Knacksap was whistling jauntily as he sat down at his desk. Then he picked up the telephone. 'Flitchbody? It's Knacksap here. I just wanted to make sure you've got everything sorted. The bodies should be with you by six this morning. Three hundred snow leopards. They'll be dead and without a scratch on them – we're going to use gas. All you've got to do is get them skinned.'

130

'Where are you going to gas them for heaven's sake?'

'Hankley Hall – it's about five miles from Wellbridge. Don't worry, it's a doddle.'

'I still don't know where you think you can get them from.'

'Well, if I told you I'd found a witch who can turn people into leopards, you wouldn't believe me. So just take it I've found someone who breeds them in secret and thinks I'm going to let them loose on the hills. And remember, Flitchbody, I want the money in cash or I'll blow the lot to kingdom come.'

He put down the phone.

Oh, God, thought Daniel. What does it mean? What shall I do?

Then something awful happened. His foot slipped and bumped against one of Mr Knacksap's walking sticks, propped in the corner of the cupboard. Daniel lunged, trying desperately to catch it – and missed. There was a frightful clatter. Then slowly . . . very slowly . . . the cupboard was opened by an unseen hand.

Heckie pulled the dragworm through the lamplit streets of Wellbridge, past Sumi's shop, past Boris's garage. Everything was shuttered; everyone slept. It was a long way to Fetlington, but the night was fresh and cool.

She was turning into Market Square when she saw, coming towards her, a furniture lorry which stopped suddenly with a squeal of brakes. Then a dumpy lady in a boiler suit got down from the cab.

It couldn't be . . . But it was!

'Dora!' said Heckie – and waited for her friend to snub her and turn away.

'Heckie!' said Dora – and waited for her friend to shout rude things at her.

There was a pause while both witches looked at each other. Then:

'Oh, Dora, I have missed you,' said Heckie.

'Oh, Heckie, I have missed *you*,' said Dora.

And then they were hugging each other and talking both at once, explaining how miserable they had been and promising that they would never, never quarrel with each other again.

All this took a little while, but then Heckie said: 'Why are you moving furniture at this time of night?'

'Well, actually . . . I was coming to see you. I was going to have a last try at being friends and I wanted to ask you if you'd take my wardrobe. It's haunted, you see, and I'm getting married and my fiancé doesn't like ghosts.'

'But of course I'll take it. Only it's so funny, Dora, because *I* was coming to see you! I wanted to have a last try at being friends and I wanted to ask you if you'd take my familiar because I'm getting married and my fiancé doesn't like dragworms!'

So then they both laughed so much they nearly fell over and said wasn't it amazing that both of them were going to get married, and then Dora opened the wardrobe and the thing came out looking white and vague and blinking worriedly – and as Dora had known she would, Heckie took to it at once.

And then Heckie unzipped the dragworm's basket and of course it was love at first sight. 'Oh, Heckie, you were always so clever with animals! The way

132

the back of him is so different from the front and yet somehow he's all of a piece!'

So now their worries were over and they could settle down to a good gossip.

'Wouldn't it be wonderful if we could visit each other every week like proper married ladies?' said Heckie.

'Oh, wouldn't it!' said Dora. 'But I'm going to live in the Lake District.'

Heckie gave a shriek of delight. 'But so am I! So am I going to live in the Lake District! Isn't it absolutely splendid! We'll be able to swap recipes and have tupperware parties and—'

She never finished her sentence. The door of the cheese wizard's shop burst open and Mr Gurgle came running across the square, still in his bedroom slippers, and as white as a sheet.

'Thank goodness!' he said, grabbing Heckie's arm. 'I thought I heard you. It's the boy... Daniel. I found him trussed up in Knacksap's cellar. He's been hit on the head and he's got brain fever, I think. He keeps talking about leopards. Three hundred snow leopards going to be gassed at Hankley Hall!'

Daniel lay on Mr Gurgle's sofa. He had lost so much blood that the room was going round and round, but when he saw Heckie, he made a desperate effort to speak.

'Leopards,' he said again. 'Three hundred... at Hankley Hall... killed.' And struggling to make her understand what he had heard: 'Flitchbody...' he began – and then fell back against the cushions.

Heckie felt his head with careful fingers. 'He must

go to hospital at once and his parents be told. Get an ambulance, Gurgle. When he's safe you can rally the others, but the boy comes first.' She turned to Dora. 'I did it,' said Heckie, and she looked like a corpse. 'I made the leopards out of the prisoners, for Li-Li to turn loose on the hills. This Flitchbody must have got wind of Li-Li's plans and kidnapped them!'

'Oh, but that's terrible, Heckie. You see one of them must be Lewis's Cousin Alfred! He went to the prison to free him. Lewis will never forgive me if Cousin Alfred gets gassed and skinned.'

'Perhaps it's not too late,' said Heckie – and both witches ran like the wind for the lorry.

# Chapter Twenty-One

It had been a splendid place once – a long, low building with towers and turrets and an avenue of lime trees. There was a statue garden with queer griffins and heraldic beasts carved in stone, and a lake and a maze – a really frightening maze, the kind with high yew hedges that could trap you for hours and hours.

But now the hall was empty and partly ruined. The people who owned Hankley couldn't afford to keep it up and then it was found that an underground river was making the back of the house sink into the ground, so nobody would buy it.

The ballroom, though, was in the front and it looked almost as it had done a hundred years ago. There were patches of damp on the ceiling and the plaster had flaked off, but the beautiful floor was still there, and the carved gallery. And now, with candles flickering in the holders and graceful shadows moving across the windows, it might have seemed as though the grand people who had danced there had come back to haunt the place in which they had once been happy.

But the creatures who moved between the pillars wore no ball gowns and carried no fans – and when they turned and wove their patterns on the floor, it was on four legs, not on two.

*

The leopards had been quiet when Heckie made them, but now it was different. The men who brought them had handled them roughly, prodding and poking with long-handled forks to send them faster down the wire tunnels and into the room. The big cats had smelled the fear in the men; their eyes glinted and they lashed each other with their tails.

A door opened high up in the gallery and a man dressed in black leather came out. His gas-mask hung by a strap round his neck and he carried a zinc-lined box which he lowered carefully on to the floor.

Sid would do anything for money. It didn't matter to him what he killed. Only the week before he'd shot two dozen horses between the eyes so that they could be sent off to be eaten. He never asked questions either. How Mr Knacksap had got hold of three hundred leopards was none of his business. All the same, as he looked down on the moving, frosty sea of beasts, he felt shivers go up and down his spine.

I wish I hadn't take it on, thought Sid.

Which was silly . . . He'd clear a thousand just for an hour's work and nothing could go wrong. The windows were sealed up; the men who drove the lorries would drag the brutes back into the vans. They had masks too. There'd be no trouble.

Better get on with it. He fitted the rubber tight over his face. Now, with his black leather suit, he looked like someone from another planet. Then he bent down and began to prise open the box.

'Stop! Stop!' A wild-haired woman had burst through the door and was running between the leopards who, strangely, parted to let her pass. 'Stop

136

at once, Flitchbody! Those aren't leopards, they're people!'

'And one of them is Cousin Alfred,' yelled a second woman, small and dumpy, in a boiler suit.

Sid straightened up. He could knock off these two loonies along with the leopards, but killing people was more of a nuisance than killing animals. There were apt to be questions asked.

'Get out of here!' he shouted, his voice muffled by the mask. 'Get out or you're for it!'

Neither of the witches moved. Heckie couldn't touch the assassin with her knuckle because there were no steps from the floor of the ballroom to the gallery. Dora couldn't look at him out of her small round eyes because he wore a mask.

They were powerless.

Sid picked up the canister of gas. The women would just have to die too. Nat and Billy could throw them in the lake afterwards.

A large leopard, scenting danger, lifted its head and roared. And high in the rafters, a family of bats fluttered out and circled the room.

The witches had always understood each other without words. Heckie knew what Dora was going to do and it hurt her, but she knew it had to be done.

'Ouch! Ow! Ooh!'

The shriek of pain came from Sid, hopping on one leg. Something as hard as a bullet had crashed down on his foot – a creepy, gargoyle thing with claws and wings made of stone. And now another one – a bat-shaped bullet hurtling down from the ceiling, missing

137

him by inches. This wasn't ordinary danger, this was something no one could endure!

Sid put down the canister and fled.

He didn't get far. Almost at once he ran into someone who was very angry. Someone whose voice made both witches prick up their ears.

'It's Li-Li,' cried Heckie. 'It's Li-Li telling off the horrible man who's been trying to kill the leopards!'

'It's Lewis,' cried Dora at the same time. 'He's come to save his Cousin Alfred!'

Mr Knacksap appeared on the gallery. He had snatched Sid's gas-mask and was heaving with temper. No one could be trusted these days. He'd have to do the job himself.

'Li-Li!' shouted Heckie. 'Thank goodness you've come!'

'Lewis!' cried Dora. 'You're just in time!'

The witches looked at each other.

'What did you call him?' asked Heckie.

'Lewis. He's my Lewis. The man I'm going to marry. What did *you* call him?'

'Li-Li. He's my Lionel. The man *I'm* going to marry.'

Then at last the scales dropped from the witches' eyes and they understood that they had been tricked and double-crossed and cheated.

And in those moments, Knacksap fixed on Sid's mask, lobbed the canister of gas high into the room – and ran.

# Chapter Twenty-Two

'Right? Is everybody ready?' said Boris Chomsky. He climbed into the basket of the black air balloon, and Sumi and the garden witch moved over to make room for him.

'Just checking the ammunition,' said Mr Gurgle importantly, from the second balloon. His balloon was grey, but it only lacked a couple of hours till dawn so it wouldn't show up too much. Joe sat beside him, and Madame Rosalia, whom no one would have recognized as Miss Witch 1965. She wore no make-up, her hair was tousled. For the past half hour she had crouched on the floor of Boris's garage, muttering the spells she'd learnt at school and thought she had forgotten. Spells to raise the wind – and the right wind. A westerly, to take them as fast as they could go to Hankley Hall.

Daniel's parents might not be able to show him much affection, but when their son was still not at home at one in the morning, the professors were frantic. They called the police, but they also went to Sumi's house, and to Joe's, to see if he was with his friends. And Sumi and Joe, running round to Heckie's in case Daniel was with the witch, had met Mr Gurgle rallying the Wickedness Hunters.

'Ammunition on board,' called Mr Gurgle. 'Ready for take-off!'

Boris put a tape of the Minister for Education saying schoolchildren needed more exams into the fuel adaptor – and the black balloon shot into the air.

Mr Gurgle inserted a cassette of the Minister for Trade saying that dumping nuclear waste was good for the fish – and the grey balloon shot upwards also.

Madame Rosalia had done her work well. The wind was keen and exactly where they wanted. Blowing them to the east and Hankley Hall!

Mr Knacksap was running, running ... stumbling along gravel paths, blundering between trees. He'd thrown off the gas-mask and the branches stung his face.

Gas-proof witches! Who would have believed it? He'd been certain that the witches had died along with the leopards when he threw the canister – but just now he'd heard them calling to each other down by the lake.

Oh, Lord, don't let them get me, prayed the furrier. Don't let me become a louse. Don't let me become a statue. And please, please don't let me become the statue of a louse!

If he could just find somewhere to hide till the witches gave up and went home. Then he could haul the leopards away – Nat and Billy should be waiting at the bottom of the drive for a signal.

But where? Where could he be safe from the women he had cheated?

Panting, gasping, almost at the end of his tether, Mr Knacksap staggered on, past fountains, down a flight of steps, tripping over roots ...

And then he saw in front of him a mass of high, dark hedges. Of course, the Hankley Maze! The first streaks of light had appeared in the east, but he'd be safe in there – no one would find him. If he was lost, so would the witches be if they tried to follow him. All he needed to do was wait till he heard them driving away, and then he'd get out all right. One just had to turn always to the left or to the right, it was perfectly easy.

Only what was that? Good heavens, WHAT WAS THAT? A thing high up in the sky. A blob . . . an Unidentified Flying Object. No, two of them. Two UFOs . . .

'It's the Martians!' screamed Mr Knacksap, weaving frantically between the hedges.

'There he is, down in the maze,' said Joe. 'We need to lose some height.'

Boris nodded and turned down the sound. In both balloons the taped gabble died to a whisper and the balloons dropped quietly to hang over the hedges of yew.

'Ready with the ammunition?'

The garden witch nodded and heaved the first of the missiles on to the edge of the basket, where Sumi steadied it and let it go.

'No! No! Don't do it!' yelled the furrier.

But the unspeakable THING was already hurtling towards him – gigantic, hideous, deformed . . . to fall not a foot away from him, spattering him with ghastly misshapen bits of itself. And now a second one – not a death-dealing cauliflower this time, but an artichoke whose spiky leaves drew blood as they gashed his cheek.

141

'Spare me! Spare me!' implored Knacksap – and a stick of celery the size of a tree caught him a glancing blow on the shoulder.

The furrier was on his knees now, gabbling and praying. But there was a fresh horror to come! From the second of the UFOs came a new menace: a rain of deadly weapons, round ones like landmines, which splattered to the ground beside him, releasing an unbearable, poisonous stink!

'No, not that one,' begged Mr Gurgle, up in the balloon. 'I'm teaching that one to skip.'

'Can't be helped,' said Joe tersely. He heaved the round, red cheese on to the rim of the basket, took aim – and fired.

This time he scored a bull's-eye. The furrier screamed once and rolled over. He was still lying on the ground, twitching, when the witches ran into the maze.

# Chapter Twenty-Three

'Have some soup,' begged Dora Mayberry, putting the tray down beside Heckie's bed. 'Please, dear. Just try a spoonful.'

'I couldn't,' said Heckie in a failing voice. 'It would choke me.'

For two weeks now she had been lying in bed in her flat above the pet shop, refusing to eat and getting paler and weaker with every day that passed.

'My heart is broken,' Heckie had explained at the beginning.

'Well, my heart is broken too,' Dora had said – but of course it had always been agreed between them that Heckie was the sensitive one and felt things more.

Dora had moved in with Heckie because her own business was sold, and she cooked for Heckie and looked after the shop and baked the dragworm's princesses, but nothing could make Heckie take any interest in life. Sumi came with nice things from her parents' shop, and Joe, and of course Daniel as soon as he was well enough. Daniel had left hospital after a few days and his parents had been so relieved that they actually took time off to make a fuss of him. But even Daniel couldn't stop Heckie lying back on her pillows and talking about death, although it was his bravery that had prevented a terrible disaster.

For the leopards had not been gassed. There was something that Mr Knacksap had forgotten if he ever knew it – and that was that Dora Mayberry had been the netball champion of the Academy.

This plump and humble witch had leapt high over a crouching leopard, caught the canister, and run – as she used to run down the pitch – to throw it safely into the lake.

The rest of that strange, exhausting night had been spent driving the leopards back to the prison, changing them back to people, and undoing the stone magic on the guards. Everyone had helped. Nat and Billy had fled, along with Sid, so it was Boris and Mr Gurgle who drove the circus vans, and the other Wickedness Hunters stood guard outside the prison till the job was done. Since the prisoners couldn't remember how they had got into the exercise yard, and the guards couldn't remember anything at all, nobody could punish anybody else, and soon the prisoners were back in their cells and quite glad to catch up on their sleep.

So everyone should now have been happy, but instead they were completely miserable – and this was because of Heckie.

When she first realized that it was Mr Knacksap who had half-killed Daniel and tried to murder three hundred people in cold blood, Heckie had felt nothing except anger and rage. But as the days passed she couldn't help remembering the chocolates with hard centres, and the red roses, and the careful way the furrier had brushed the crumbs off his trousers as they picnicked above the gas works – and

144

she felt so sad that really there seemed no point in staying alive.

And while Heckie faded away, the power of her magic grew weaker too and very strange things happened in the zoo. The warthog had to be taken out of her cage and sent to the veterinary hospital because an odd fleshy bulge, just like a human leg, had appeared on her back end, and the unusual fish began to gasp and come up for air. The others tried to keep news of these things from Heckie, but they were all very worried indeed.

'I really think I ought to call the doctor,' said Dora now, taking away the tray with Heckie's untasted soup.'

'There's nothing he can do,' said Heckie dramatically. 'I'm better off dead.'

So poor Dora shuffled off and Heckie lay back on the pillow and thought about her ruined life and what she wanted put on her tombstone. She had decided on: HERE LIES HECATE TENBURY-SMITH WHO MEANT WELL BUT GOT EVERYTHING WRONG, when she heard a voice somewhere in the room.

'Quite honestly,' it said, 'I think this has gone on long enough.'

Heckie opened her eyes. All her visitors had gone. Dora was in the kitchen. Then she looked down, and there was the dragworm sitting in his basket and looking peeved.

'But you can't speak!' she said, amazed.

'I never said I *couldn't*,' said the dragworm. 'I *didn't* because there's too much conversation in the world already. Babble, babble all day long. But to

145

see you going on like this just turns me right off. And all for a man who, to say the least, is thoroughly vulgar. Furthermore, I have no wish to turn back into a duck. Being a duck was the most boring thing that ever happened to me.'

'But surely—'

The dragworm rose from the basket and slithered over to the bed. 'There,' he said, lifting his tail. 'On the fifth bulge from the end. *Feathers*.'

'Oh, *dear*!'

'And more to come, I shouldn't wonder. Everything's going to pieces. I wouldn't be surprised if that mouse you made in the bank hasn't got himself a machine-gun by now. So I suggest you pull yourself together and forget that creep. The smell of his toilet water . . .'

Heckie had propped herself on one elbow. 'You didn't like it?'

'*Like* it? You must be joking!'

'Perhaps it was a little strong,' Heckie agreed. 'But I don't really know what to do with my life any more. I feel such a failure.'

'Well, for a start you can eat something. As for me, I could do with a change. What's with this Paradise Cottage there was all that fuss about?'

# Chapter Twenty-Four

There is nothing like country air for mending broken hearts, and it was not long before Heckie and Dora realized that marriage would not have suited them. However hard gentlemen try, they always seem to snore in bed, their underclothes need washing and they throw their socks on to the floor.

And Paradise Cottage was exactly the kind of home the witches had dreamt of. Mr Knacksap had cut the picture out of a house agent's catalogue and when Heckie and Dora went up to the Lake District to enquire, they found that it was still for sale. So they bought it with the money from both their businesses and settled down to be proper country ladies.

Heckie did not often turn people into animals now; she liked to Do Good more quietly, healing the wounded sheep she sometimes met on her walks, or comforting a cow that was having trouble with its calf. Dora, too, preferred just to help with the stonework of the church, adding noses to chipped statues or building up the missing toes on tombstones. Country people are used to seeing strange creatures and they could take the dragworm out without having to zip him in to his basket, and he and the spirit in the wardrobe had become firm friends.

But though they were so happy in the country, the witches had been looking forward for weeks to

Daniel's first visit, and they had planned a special surprise. He arrived on a beautiful frosty afternoon at the little station beside the lake, but they were not there to meet him. Instead, they sent a friendly taxi driver who took Daniel up the steep winding lane and left him at the garden gate. The front door of the cottage was open, but when Daniel knocked there was at first no answer. He could see two bats hanging upside down on the umbrella stand – the bats that had fallen on Sid in the ballroom, which they had changed back and adopted – but no sign of the witches.

'Is anybody there?' he called.

There was the sound of rustling and whispering, and then Heckie's voice.

'This way, Daniel. We're in here!'

Daniel pushed open the door of the dining-room. The table was set for a party, with candles burning in silver holders, and a bright fire danced in the grate.

But it was the witches themselves who really caught Daniel's attention.

Both of them wore their hats – the hats they had quarrelled about so stupidly a year ago. The snakes were bigger now – the Black Mamba had grown enough to tie in a double bow which hung enchantingly over Heckie's eyes and nestled on Dora's serious forehead. The Ribbon Snakes on the crown shimmered and flickered and the King Snakes, with their brilliant red bands, caught the fire from the lamp.

'We wanted to surprise you,' said Heckie, holding out her arms.

148

'You look beautiful,' said Daniel. 'Absolutely *beautiful*!' and went forward to hug them both.

But that was not the end of it. When Daniel took his place at the table, he found a small tank beside his plate – and inside it, a hat of his own!

'We made it for you,' said Heckie. 'It's more of a cap, really, like sportsmen wear.'

'We do hope that you will like it,' put in Dora. 'The colours are suitable for gentlemen, we feel.'

There was a time when Daniel would have been worried about putting his hand into a tank of writhing snakes and placing them on his head – but that time was past. And when he went over to the mirror, he could not stop smiling, for really he had never worn anything that suited him so well. The witches had used young green pythons which brought out the colour of Daniel's eyes, and in the place where fishermen sometimes stuck feathered flies, the bright head of a cobra flickered and swayed.

With everyone so smart, it couldn't help being a lovely party. The food was delicious and the tea, of course, was perfect because of Daniel's present – the machine that dropped exactly the right number of tea-bags into the pot. But when they had eaten, and Daniel had given them the messages from Joe and Sumi, who were coming to stay at Easter, the witches put down their cups and sighed.

'Tell us, dear,' said Heckie. 'How is . . . *he*?'

'Yes, how *is* . . . he?' asked Dora.

'Well, I haven't seen him myself because they don't let children into the prison,' said Daniel. 'But Sumi's mother goes sometimes. She says he doesn't like the food, but the other prisoners don't bully him or anything. And they're teaching him to sew mailbags which must be useful, I suppose?'

For Mr Knacksap had not ended up as a statue or a louse. The witches had planned to do dreadful things to him, but when they found him in the maze, felled by cheese, they had looked at each other and left him where he was. They had both loved him truly and though they knew what an evil man he was, they could not bring themselves to use their magic powers against him.

So they had dropped a note in at the police station, and when the police reached him with their tracker dogs, they had taken him straight to the police station and charged him with attacking Daniel. And when they began to ask questions, they found a lot more things that he had done: bouncing cheques, cheating on his income tax, embezzling – and now he was Prisoner Number 301 in Wellbridge jail.

The rest of the evening passed in a flash and then it was bedtime.

'Am I sleeping in the room with the wardrobe?' Daniel asked hopefully.

'Of course, dear,' said Heckie.

When he had brushed his teeth and put on his pyjamas and placed the tank with his hat in it on a chair where he could see it first thing in the morning, Daniel opened the window and drank in the cool, fresh country air. He was much happier now in the tall, grey house in Wellbridge. His parents had not forgotten the shock of finding their son in hospital with his head in bandages. They nagged him less and tried to spend more time with him, and he knew

150

that, in their own way, they loved him. But home for him would always be where Heckie was, and as he burrowed down between the sheets, he sighed with contentment because there were days and days of the holidays still to come.

He was just closing his eyes when he heard the wood spirit's reedy little voice.

'Don't chop—' it began.

And then the dragworm, firm and strict, like an uncle. 'Now that's enough. I don't want to hear another word about chopping. Go to sleep.'

'Will you tell me a story, then?'

'Oh, all right.'

There was a rustle while the spirit settled itself among the coathangers.

'Once upon a time,' began the dragworm, 'there was a fierce and mighty dragon.'

'Like you?' asked the wood spirit.

'Like me,' agreed the dragworm. 'In the spring this dragon flew up to heaven and in the autumn he plunged down into the sea, but in the winter he lived in a crystal cave high on a bare and lonely rock . . .'

It was a beautiful story with everything in it that a story should have: knights in armour and princesses and noble deeds. But long before everyone lived happily ever after, Daniel was asleep.

Turn the page for an extract from

# MOUNTWOOD SCHOOL FOR GHOSTS

by exciting new storytelling talent

## TOBY IBBOTSON

Based on an original idea by his mother, the late, great

## EVA IBBOTSON

# Percy

The next day when Daniel came home from school, his new neighbours had arrived. They were called Mr and Mrs Bosse-Lynch, and Daniel's Great-Aunt Joyce, who had been spying from her window all day, was very satisfied. They had the right sort of car, and the right sort of clothes, and Mr Bosse-Lynch had started trimming the hedge immediately. Then two ladies from the town had arrived to clean the house, and Great-Aunt Joyce had heard Mrs Bosse-Lynch telling them what to do before they had even got through the door.

That night, when Daniel had put his light out and lay in the darkness waiting for sleep, he heard something. At first he thought that it must be a pigeon under the slates. But it wasn't the right cooing and scratching noise that pigeons made. It seemed to be coming from the wall beside his bed. On the other side of the wall, he knew, was an attic room just like his in the house next door. The noise was more a snuffling or gulping kind of noise. He sat up and put his ear to the wall. Now he could hear quite clearly. He heard stifled sobs, and sniffs. Someone was crying.

Daniel lay down again and tried to think. Perhaps Mrs Bosse-Lynch was secretly a very tragic person, with a horrible sad secret that she crept up to the attic and cried about at night. He hoped not, because he didn't want to feel sorry for someone whom horrid Great-Aunt Joyce approved of. But it was far more likely that they had a prisoner in the attic. They had kidnapped someone, probably a rich man's daughter, and sneaked her into the house. Soon they would cut off her ear and send it to the desperate parents. On the other hand, it could be a poor mad relation whom they didn't want anybody to know about. Daniel's friend Charlotte had read a book about someone like that. It was called *Jane Eyre* and was one of her absolute favourites.

Either way, Daniel had to make contact. He sat up again and knocked three times on the wall. The sniffling stopped.

'Hello, who's there?' he called. 'Do you need help?'

Still there was no sound. But then part of the wall slowly went soft and bulgy. The bulge got bigger, and separated itself from the wall. It was swirly and colourless, almost transparent. Then parts of it started taking shape, a hand appeared here, a leg there. The air in the room was suddenly icy cold, and in front of Daniel stood a small boy in a nightshirt, with golden curls and big weepy eyes.

'You are a ghost, aren't you?' said Daniel. 'I thought you were someone in trouble.'

'I am someone in trouble,' said the ghost, and huge ghostly tears started to roll down its cheeks. 'I am someone in terrible trouble.'

'I think I saw when you came,' said Daniel. 'You were in the removal van.'

'Yes, I was,' said the ghost. 'It wasn't a bus.' The tears rolled ever faster down its pale cheeks.

'Of course it wasn't a bus, it was a removal van.'

'But I thought it was,' gulped the ghost. 'And I don't know where I am and I don't know where Father and Mother are and—'

'Please try to stop crying,' said Daniel. 'And keep your voice down or you'll wake Great-Aunt Joyce.'

The ghost was obviously a young child, and seemed to be working himself into hysterics. 'If you calm down and tell me about it, I might be able to help.'

Daniel was secretly a bit disappointed. Ever since the arrival of the removal van he had been hoping for something really shockingly ghastly, perhaps a leering headless skeleton or a viciously grinning ghost murderer who dissolved his victims in acid. Anything really that would scare Great-Aunt Joyce to death, or at least make her flee from Markham Street and never return. But if she came up now and saw this weeping boy, she would probably just slap him and shoo him out.

However, even a small sad ghost is better than no ghost at all, and Daniel was a kind person and more than willing to sort out his problems if he could.

'You'd better tell me the whole story,' he said, and Perceval, for that was his name, came and sat on the bed and began.

Percy told his story with lots of pauses for miserable sniffing and cries of 'Oh, what am I to do?' and 'I shall be alone forever!', so it took him quite a long time.

Percy and his parents, Ronald and Iphigenia, had materialized in good time at the service station, where they had met up with Cousin Vera and the other ghosts and spectres who had applied for Mountwood School for Ghosts. There was quite a crowd milling about the parking bay where the bus was to pick them up. Some of them were old acquaintances, and they hung about, chatting, catching up on each other's news. After a while, when the bus still hadn't come, Percy had got bored and wandered off. There were lots of great big lorries standing silent and dark in the parking area. Percy glided among them, peeping in sometimes to look at the drivers snoring in their cabs. They had little beds with curtains, which reminded Percy of when he had been alive and his mother had read poetry to him before he went to sleep. His favourite one had started, 'Where the bee sucks there suck I.'

When Percy got back to the pick-up place, he saw a bus standing in the parking bay, revving its engine. There were no ghosts to be seen. He cried, 'Help, help, wait for me! Don't leave without me!' and threw himself through the side of the bus just as it drew away and rumbled off into the night.

'But it wasn't a bus,' said Percy sadly, looking with at Daniel with tragic eyes. 'The bus had already left.'

'Well, why didn't your parents wait for you? They must have been worried sick when you didn't show up.'

'I don't know, I don't know. I have been aba . . . adn . . .'

'Abandoned.'

'Y-y-yes. Like the Babes in the Wood.' Percy collapsed in hopeless weeping.

When he had recovered slightly Daniel said, 'I still don't see how you could mistake a removal van for a bus.'

'But I've never *been* on a bus. And it had words on the side like where we were going.'

'What do you mean?'

But Percy could speak no more. With a final wail

of 'Poor me! Oh, sad unhappy me!' he threw himself face down on the bed.

Daniel heard Great-Aunt Joyce's bedroom door opening, and her tread on the stair.

'That's done it,' he said.

'I'll disappear,' said Percy. 'I'm quite good at it.' And he started to fade, vanishing just as Great-Aunt Joyce appeared in the doorway.

Daniel turned on his bedside light. Great-Aunt Joyce was wearing a flannel dressing gown and tartan slippers, and her hair was in curlers. She looked very angry, and peered around the room.

'Really, Daniel, this is appalling. What on earth is going on? I must have silence after my pill. I shall be speaking to your father.'

'Oh, it's you, Great-Aunt Joyce. I was having a terrible nightmare.'

'Were you now?' said Great-Aunt Joyce suspiciously, and it seemed to Daniel that she stared intently at the exact spot where Percy had just vanished. 'A nightmare, was it? That's what comes of not chewing your food properly. Poor digestion.'

When she had gone, a small voice spoke from the empty bed.

'She doesn't seem very nice,' said Percy.

'She isn't. We'll have to be absolutely quiet now, Percy. We'll talk about this tomorrow.'

# THE BEASTS OF CLAWSTONE CASTLE

# EVA IBBOTSON

*'They ought to be in the country,' said Mrs Hamilton.*
*'It's where children ought to be.'*

When Madlyn Hamilton and her younger brother
Rollo are sent by their mother to stay with their
Uncle George at crumbling Clawstone Castle, they
can see that action is needed before the castle falls
down completely! With the help of a team of
scary ghosts – including Mr Smith, a one-eyed
skeleton, and Brenda the Bloodstained Bride – they
hatch a spooky plan to save their new home. But
with a sinister scientist after the estate's prize
cattle, money might not be enough to save the
mysterious white beasts of Clawstone Castle . . .

# THE SECRET OF PLATFORM 13

## EVA IBBOTSON

*'Well, this is it!' said Ernie Hobbs, floating past the boarded-up Left Luggage Office and coming to rest on an old mailbag. 'This is the day!'*

Platform 13 at King's Cross Station hides a remarkable secret. Every nine years a doorway opens to an amazing, fantastical island and its occupants come visiting. But the last time the doorway was open the island's baby prince was stolen from the streets of London. Now, nine years later, a rescue party, led by a wizard and an ogre, is back to find him and bring him home. But the gentle prince seems to have become a spoilt rich boy, and he doesn't believe in magic and *doesn't* want to go home. Can they rescue him before the doorway disappears forever?

# WHICH WITCH?

# EVA IBBOTSON

*'And remember,' he said, throwing out his arms, 'that what I am looking for is power, wickedness and evil. Darkness is All!'*

Arriman the Awful, feared Wizard of the North, is searching for a monstrous witch with the darkest powers and is holding a sorcery competition to discover which witch is the most fiendish. Glamorous Madame Olympia conjures up a thousand plague-bearing rats, while Belladonna, the white witch, desperately wants to be a wicked enchantress, but only manages to produce flowers not snakes. Can she become more devilish than all the other witches?

# MONSTER MISSION

# EVA IBBOTSON

*'We must kidnap some children,' announced Aunt Etta.*
*'Young, strong ones. It will be dangerous,*
*but it must be done.'*

Three children – Minette, Fabio and Lambert –
are stolen and taken away to a bizarre island, home
to mermaids, the strange and enormous boobrie
bird, selkies and the legendary kraken.
But soon the children find themselves in great
danger as the island is under siege from a wicked
man with plans to use these extraordinary
creatures to make money. Can the children
save themselves and their new friends?

# THIS BOOK COULD HELP

In aid of

**mind**

for better mental health

All royalties from the sale of this book
(a minimum of £10,000) will be donated
to Mind, a registered charity in England
and Wales (charity number 219830)

# THIS BOOK COULD HELP

## THE MEN'S HEAD SPACE MANUAL

### ROTIMI AKINSETE

Michael O'Mara Books Limited

First published in Great Britain in 2019 by
Michael O'Mara Books Limited
9 Lion Yard
Tremadoc Road
London SW4 7NQ

A CIP catalogue record for this book is available from the British Library.

Papers used by Michael O'Mara Books Limited are natural, recyclable products
made from wood grown in sustainable forests. The manufacturing processes
conform to the environmental regulations of the country of origin.

ISBN: 978-1-78929-131-5 in paperback print format
ISBN: 978-1-78929-145-2 in ebook format

1 2 3 4 5 6 7 8 9 10

www.mombooks.com

Cover design by Ana Bjezancevic
Designed by Blok Graphic, London

Thanks to the University of Surrey and University of Exeter for the 'Relax' exercises.
Thanks to the men who donated their words (identities have been changed).

Printed and bound in Europe.

# Contents

# Introduction

We often hear about needing to maintain our physical health: eat well, exercise and so on, but, frankly, our head space doesn't get the same consideration. For men in particular, it's often suggested that we ought to have some magical mental world that's infinitely resilient, immovable, positive, sure of itself – that we should be able to cope with everything that life throws at us. I've yet to meet this person. In fact, I don't know anyone who doesn't have times when they find life a battle.

**But the sad fact is that many more men than women don't want to open up about having problems because they believe that will mean that *they* are the problem.**

It's not surprising when you consider the barrage of messages and the language aimed at men about how we ought to be. We are told to 'man up' and that 'boys don't cry' – and a load of other absurd and desperately unhelpful clichés that hold us back from expressing ourselves and holding on to our individuality. We're surrounded by these messages, on TV, on social media, in advertising and, no matter how well-intentioned, from our friends and family. I've experienced it myself, growing up. For example, I remember trying to explain that I wanted to study social work or psychology or something in the caring professions and being told: 'Are you a man or are you a woman?', 'Do something useful, like law or engineering', and 'Make your mother proud and be a doctor!'

**Who wouldn't struggle to be themselves when they're confronted with this attitude?**

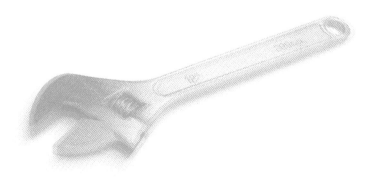

These messages and images can be really powerful and potentially dangerous when they are left to build and build. Sadly, many men will decide to end their life rather than seek help. Around the world, suicide is one of the biggest killers of men under the age of forty-five. In fact, in the UK, it is the biggest killer. And many more men are struggling to cope and feeling alone.

I work with men of all ages and all sorts of backgrounds, and the most common reason for not seeking help is the stigma that is still attached to mental health concerns. Many men fear judgement for seeking support or worry they should deal with their problems themselves rather than burden loved ones.

**As a result, when men are feeling low, frightened, depressed, strung out or anxious, they often try to deal with it alone.**

Thankfully, things are changing. More men are talking about their own experiences. In particular, men in the media spotlight are coming forward and sharing their stories, refuting the lie that men don't (and, even worse, shouldn't) build, manage and struggle with their internal world. While it's clear that seeking help when you're really struggling is important – and it is incredibly important – regular maintenance is something we should *all* try to do. It's about respecting what you as a human need to function. The exercises in this book are like the mental equivalent of eating your vegetables and visiting the gym (incidentally, these things all help your head space too). They are designed to be helpful whatever challenges you are facing right now.

To be honest, most of the advice in this book applies to anyone. But I want to speak to men in particular because it's really important that you know it applies to you. I've heard men being told to 'kick depression in the balls', 'show anxiety who's boss' and so on. The idea that men can dominate mental health if only they're strong enough (because, you know, that's what men do) is ridiculous. Looking after your mind is not like finally scaling Everest or K2, it's not something to 'conquer'.

There are some fascinating ongoing and positive conversations going on in the world about what it means to be a man, aiming to change attitudes so that men are no longer dictated to about who they ought to be, and that can only be a good thing. In the meantime, this book is a practical starting point for taking care of your head space, to help you get to know yourself better, to help build your resilience and resourcefulness and to increase your satisfaction with life.

*This Book Could Help* is designed to give you some tools you can use. It will hopefully give you more confidence if you have self-doubt; it might give you a different perspective if you have suffered a great loss; it may help you grow beyond that failure you keep reminding yourself about. Or maybe it will just help you find a little peace. Different people are helped by different things. There is no ten-step programme that will work for everyone. In fact, there are eleven sections in this book, designed to build upon one another – but if there are sections that are more relevant to you right now, feel free to just dip in and out. Make the changes you want to make. That's the only way any of this works.

# Let's begin

*This Book Could Help* is published by Michael O'Mara Books to raise awareness for Mind, the mental health charity. All royalties from the sale of this book (a minimum of £10,000) will be donated to Mind, a registered charity in England (no. 219830) and a registered company (no. 424348) in England and Wales.

For information on how to contact Mind, see the 'Resources' section near the back of the book.

In aid of
for better mental health

# Part One:

# Who do you think you are?

All of us, without exception, have ideas about who we are as people and how we think others see us: what our strengths and weaknesses are, what we like or don't like, what matters to us. And these ideas can have a lot of power: they can influence how we live our lives, what we expect of ourselves, how we make decisions and how we treat ourselves.

——

**Some of your ideas about yourself are going to be helpful, others not so much.**

**The fact is that you weren't born with these ideas, you learned them. As a social animal you've been surrounded by messages telling you how you ought to be from day one – and when it comes to being a man, the mould is pretty tight – this means that some of these ideas aren't going to have come from you.**

━━━━━

The thing is, however they come to you, these ideas we have can and do change, and you can have a say in where they go. You may have already noticed it. I remember that I used to define myself as a provider and would work three jobs and attend various committees in order to bring home the bacon and make a name for myself. When I started questioning it, I realized that I was doing myself real physical and mental damage by trying too hard to be a person that really wasn't me. Now I see myself as someone who prioritizes quality time with his family, and I'm confident that this time it is the real me. These shifts happen, all the time. They may not be predictable, and they may take time, but they do show that things aren't as set in stone as they can sometimes seem.

# Ten words

If you had to describe yourself in ten words, what would they be? That probably sounds like the beginning of some cringe-inducing job interview, but trust me, it's important.

If you've never thought about it before, the words on the page opposite might be a starting point. Or you could think about completing the sentence:

## 'I am someone who ...'

Once you have a clear and honest idea of at least some of the things that you believe about yourself, ask yourself, which of them propel you forward? Which hold you back? Did you always believe them about yourself? How have they changed over time? Where did these beliefs come from?

You probably won't know the answers to all of these questions (and you don't need to). The key here is to start thinking about how you see yourself and how this impacts your life. Because if you don't want to define yourself in this way, you don't have to. It's up to you.

# I am...

- ☐ strong
- ☐ weak
- ☐ decisive
- ☑ loyal
- ☐ bold
- ☑ a listener
- ☐ competitive
- ☑ sensitive
- ☑ a failure
- ☐ a husband
- ☐ a success
- ☐ a partner
- ☐ a manager
- ☐ a colleague
- ☑ a neighbour
- ☐ a sports-lover
- ☐ an employer
- ☑ a consumer
- ☑ spiritual
- ☐ fit
- ☐ attractive
- ☑ a reader
- ☑ a writer
- ☑ unfit
- ☐ a provider
- ☐ an activist
- ☐ rich

- ☑ poor
- ☐ an employee
- ☐ a peacemaker
- ☐ a soulmate
- ☐ a sportsman
- ☐ a politician
- ☐ a mentor
- ☐ an explorer
- ☑ critical
- ☑ a music-lover
- ☐ a freedom fighter
- ☑ a joker
- ☐ organized
- ☐ a businessman
- ☑ a gentleman
- ☐ a player
- ☑ a comedian
- ☑ a listener
- ☐ a networker
- ☐ a leader
- ☑ a follower
- ☐ resourceful
- ☐ practical
- ☐ ambitious
- ☑ kind
- ☐ selfish
- ☐ vain

- ☑ easy-going
- ☐ uptight
- ☐ aggressive
- ☑ patient
- ☐ ruthless
- ☐ mature
- ☑ immature
- ☑ conscientious
- ☑ lazy
- ☐ responsible
- ☐ reckless
- ☑ faithful
- ☑ honest
- ☑ brave
- ☐ cunning
- ☐ fake
- ☑ authentic
- ☑ straightforward
- ☑ eccentric
- ☐ conventional
- ☑ open-minded
- ☐ intolerant
- ☐ a dad
- ☑ a brother
- ☑ a son
- ☐ an uncle
- ☑ a man

# "How would I describe myself?

Probably more than anything else, as a dad. That's the thing that immediately comes to mind.

It's who I am, and I'm really proud of it.

It's not always easy, but thinking that I'm a good dad makes me feel good.

**Len, 43, dad**

# Running commentary

All of us have a soundtrack running in our minds, a running commentary on what we're doing. You do, too, and you might not even know it's happening. Sometimes it's just you observing the world around you, but often it's a commentary about yourself: judging what you've done, how you handled something, how you sounded, how you looked ...

What does your running commentary sound like? For example, if you make a mistake, do you tend to beat

yourself up, judge yourself harshly, blame yourself? Or is it more like, 'Ah well, better luck next time'? How about more general situations? Are you often critical or often supportive of how you acted? Now ask yourself, would you talk to a good friend like that? Chances are you wouldn't – so try not to talk to yourself like that either.

If you manage to catch that critical commentary as it starts up, try to interrupt it and replace it with a supportive one. Be on your side.

'When I fuck up, my response is, "You fucking idiot!" If I spoke to my friends like I used to talk to myself, I would have no friends.

Make sure the words you speak to yourself are loving, supportive and nourishing. Start the work of being your own best friend.'

**Wentworth Miller, actor**

# What's working?

Help stop your negative running commentary by pausing to appreciate your achievements. These could be things you do every day – for some people, getting up in the morning deserves acknowledgement, for others being on time for work, going for a run, getting the kids to school or helping someone out is something to feel good about.

## Whatever it is, recognize the part you played in it.

You don't have to give yourself a gold sticker – but you could think about rewarding yourself in some way, like keeping reminders of your more significant triumphs (whatever they might be). Take the tradition of football players who score hat-tricks – they get to keep the match ball and take the team out to celebrate.

Remember, no one wins big every day, but everyone achieves something because in every situation, organization, business or community, something works. Don't let it go unrecognized.

# Part Two:

# Level vibes

Emotions get a bad rap. People often talk about being emotional as if it means being weak or soft. But this is clearly nonsense. In terms of evolution, emotions are one of the reasons that human beings are top of the species pile. It's because we have emotions that we are so successful at innovating, exploring, persevering and surviving. Our emotions are telling us something we need to know, they work as short cuts to intelligent behaviour. And the bottom line is that they are a vital part of being human.

For men, there seem to be just a handful of emotions that are deemed acceptable to admit to: happiness, anger and sometimes sadness, when it's seen as being the result of something truly tragic like a bereavement.

**But for many of us, it's not OK to admit to experiencing other incredibly common feelings, like insecurity or anxiety.**

But whether we like it or not, that doesn't stop those feelings being there. While you can push them down and try to ignore them, or turn them into something else (like getting angry when in fact you're feeling sad), the truth is that they aren't going anywhere – and for a good reason: you need them in order to function.

# Name it

If you've had a lifetime of actively avoiding your feelings (and even when you haven't) it can be a challenge to start paying them attention. Sometimes you might not know how you're feeling, or you might not have the words to describe it, which can be incredibly frustrating. Or the language that you do have might not feel like it's enough. For instance, you might say that you're 'upset'. But what is 'upset'? Upset can mean different things at different times. It can mean angry or sad or frustrated, lonely or insecure, or lots of other things.

> **Like anything worth doing, accurately describing how you're feeling – 'naming your emotions' – takes practice.**

Think of it as like learning a new language – like when your mind first made the connection between a word and your experience of it. For example, you had to see a ball before you knew what 'ball' actually meant, right?

On the page opposite, there's a list of words that might jog your thoughts. It might be that you're already well practised in identifying your feelings, but, equally, you might never have really thought about a lot of them before (you wouldn't be alone in that, trust me!). Take a few minutes to really consider a few of them and what they mean. Do any of them describe what you're feeling right now?

| | | |
|---|---|---|
| ☑ happy | ☐ disrespected | ☐ naive |
| ☐ sad | ☑ proud | ☑ sensitive |
| ☐ affected | ☑ hopeful | ☑ naughty |
| ☐ abandoned | ☑ grateful | ☐ uneducated |
| ☐ vexed | ☑ inspired | ☐ unworthy |
| ☐ withdrawn | ☑ relieved | ☐ confused |
| ☑ extroverted | ☑ satisfied | ☐ bad-tempered |
| ☐ introverted | ☑ curious | ☐ furious |
| ☑ sociable | ☐ belittled | ☐ used |
| ☑ clever | ☐ fraught | ☑ content |
| ☐ moody | ☐ ecstatic | ☑ needy |
| ☐ fed up | ☐ small | ☑ enthusiastic |
| ☐ squeamish | ☐ angry | ☐ challenged |
| ☐ soft | ☐ exploited | ☐ invisible |
| ☑ vulnerable | ☐ patronized | ☐ weak |
| ☑ mindful | ☐ abused | ☐ strong |
| ☑ thoughtful | ☑ enlightened | ☐ ugly |
| ☐ frustrated | ☑ lazy | ☑ obsessive |

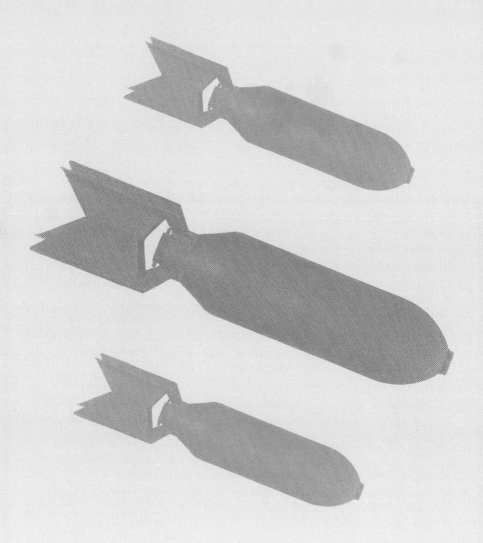

# When my mum died, I was just so angry all the time.

# Somehow it was easier to be angry, than to be sad.

**Alex, 28, prison officer**

# Letting it all hang out

If you struggle to express your emotions, it can be helpful to take stock of the images of men that surround you and how they might be affecting you. For instance, when was the last time you saw a man cry? In a film? On TV? What about the men among your friends? Family? Have you *ever* seen them cry?

There's a saying: 'If you can see it, you can be it.' In other words, if the people surrounding you don't tend to show how they're feeling then you're less likely to feel comfortable doing it yourself. And this is especially the case for people you consider to be like you, or people you aspire to be like.

**First of all, give yourself a break.**

Undoing centuries of male conditioning is going to feel like an uphill climb at first. But, look a bit harder. Are there some situations – that you don't even think about – where you see men finding ways of letting out their emotions? For some, it'll be in the stands at sports stadiums, either doing somersaults when their team does well – or bawling their eyes out when they don't. Surveys have also recently shown that behind closed doors men will cry around thirty times a year. There are more indirect ways as well, such as with physical exercise, which can help release some of the tension behind pent up emotions.

**You might already be doing things that help you let off steam. If you are, get wise to them so that you can use them when you need to.**

# Leaking

If we don't acknowledge and do something with our pain, it tends to find a way out on its own, and this can come in many forms. Some people develop a negative running commentary (see page 18), others might use drink or drugs, or find themselves lashing out verbally or physically. It's different for different people.

If you're someone who tends to bottle things up it might be worth looking at your own life in case there's a leak that's influencing the way you behave, feel or think.

'I didn't realize it at the time, but all my fears around losing my job and not talking about it to anyone were coming out in doubles and triples at the bar. When I finally confided in my partner, I noticed that I stopped reaching for the booze.'

**Ben, 42, lawyer**

# Do you have a leak?

# Part Three:

# Talk that talk

When somebody asks you how you are doing, what do you say? Most of us tend to give a fairly non-committal, automatic answer like, 'All right', 'Yeah, good', 'Fine' – even if life is anything but. It's a tough habit to break, for anyone. Somehow, admitting that you aren't OK feels uncomfortable.

**But when you feel stressed, down, worried, angry, excited, sad, who do you tell?**

What about if something happens to you at work, on the street, with your health, with your friends or family, or with your partner?

The truth is that many, if not most, of us avoid talking about what is going on – and it can also be seen as going against ingrained ideas of how men ought to be.

———

**I often hear men say that they feel as if they should be able to deal with stuff on their own; that they don't want to be a burden to anyone; that they don't want to appear weak.**

———

As a result, you can end up keeping all of these things to yourself. And if you are going through a hard time then it can become like a weight that just gets heavier and heavier.

# Why not?

If you're comfortable with talking about what's happening in your life, then great – crack on! But if you're not, maybe it's time to start questioning the reasons for that. Maybe you just don't see yourself as that kind of person (it might be worth flicking back to the 'Ten words' exercise to think further about this), or maybe it's a question of having never done it before, worrying about how people will take it, how they will see you. Maybe it's an alien experience and you don't know where to start?

When you've begun to get a handle on what's holding you back, try asking: are these reasons worth it? Is there a way that I can overcome them? How can I start talking?

And don't forget to be realistic. If you've spent your whole life feeling this way, then suddenly rocking up at your friend's house and unloading your deepest, darkest feelings is probably not going to happen, but perhaps you could write one small thing down in a text message.

One way to get used to the idea of talking is to listen to other people doing it. The good news is that more and more men are sharing their own stories and struggles.

From those in the spotlight, like comedians, athletes, actors and politicians, to men who aren't famous – in the form of blogs, articles, podcasts and YouTube videos. Even TV drama is getting in on the act, showing how important 'talking therapy' is to the most unlikely of characters. Remember the US crime drama *The Sopranos,* where the main character Tony Soprano regularly meets with his female therapist to help balance his multi-layered difficulties? A tough mafia guy gradually getting to grips with his feelings. Brilliant.

> **What that show said to me is that it doesn't matter what kind of man you think you are – talking is for everyone.**

I was sitting at the kitchen table when it all came out. There was a moment's silence afterwards, when I was thinking,

"What have I done!"

# But then my brother just said: "Me too, Mo, me too."

# You could have knocked me over with a feather.

**Mohammad, 20, student**

# Ask yourself

If you're not ready to talk to someone else yet, or even if you are, talking to yourself can help get your head straight on what life is like for you right now. Asking yourself questions can be a good start. The key is to be honest, even if you don't like the answer. It's a way of getting to grips with what's bothering you, or what's going well for you, and will help you think about what to do about it. On the page opposite there are some questions you could consider.

## Write it down

Writing down what's on your mind – worries, stresses and so on – can be incredibly cathartic. And it doesn't have to mean keeping a journal (although, a lot of people do find this helpful – Winston Churchill, Mark Twain and Bruce Lee were big journal-keepers, for example). Just the process of writing, getting what's going on inside your head out onto paper, is where the relief comes. You can even throw away the paper afterwards if you want.

**1** How well am I sleeping?

**2** Am I feeling a bit low or fed up a lot of the time?

**3** Am I lacking enthusiasm for things I normally love doing?

**4** Am I more irritable than usual?

**5** Are people saying to me that I'm not my usual self?

**6** Am I finding it hard to be on top of things at work?

**7** Am I having difficulties in a significant relationship?

**8** Is sex difficult in some way lately?

**9** Do I sometimes feel like losing my temper and lashing out?

**10** Do I find myself avoiding people/company?

# Who to talk to

There's no one answer to this. It depends on who is in your life and what you want to talk about. Remember, talking doesn't have to mean jumping straight in at the deep end.

## If you're not used to it, start off light and build up.

Is there someone you trust and who you feel close to? Perhaps a friend or family member? If you do open up to your friends, you might be surprised by how many feel the same way but did not want to be the first to admit it. I've heard so many men confess to me that they wish they'd started talking earlier.

You could also chat to your doctor – they're often a good first port of call as they can help you work out what's going on for you and let you know what's on offer in your local area. Alternatively, you can read up online about the different kinds of guidance and help that's out there. Flip to the 'Resources' section at the back of the book for more information.

## Counselling

I've met a lot of people who feel that counselling isn't for them, that their problems don't deserve a counsellor's attention, or that counselling is all about wading through your childhood and interpreting dreams. But the truth is, counselling is about giving you a space in which you can talk through what's going on with you – get stuff off your chest and figure out how to move forwards.

# It can help you move forward when you feel stuck.

A counsellor is a trained professional who will not judge you, will prioritize confidentiality, and who will work with you to achieve goals that you set. A counsellor won't tell you what to do, they will help you reach a point where those goals are comfortably within your grasp, and will respect the decisions you make as you go through that process. There are many different types of counselling (including both one-to-one or in a group). But whatever you decide to do, it's helpful to know that it's out there should you want it.

# Be the change

Could you be the change you want to see? This means, if you feel able to, helping others around you – friends, family, kids, partner, co-workers – to talk about the things which may be bothering them.

## Small things can make the difference.

Like asking your friend how he is and really listening to the answer. Or, if you notice someone is going through a tough time, ask them about it; if the answer is brief, follow it up with another question that shows you're genuinely interested in how they are.

Giving someone the opportunity to talk can make the difference between them sharing what's going on and getting some relief and support, or staying silent and carrying it on their own. And they might not go for it first time, but persevering and making them feel they can open up if they want to sends them a clear message that you're there and ready to listen.

## Listening

Good, active listening can be a tough skill to learn, which is why there are professional training courses designed to teach people how to do it. I know it probably doesn't sound like rocket science, but the practice can be harder than you think. Here are some pointers:

**Show that you're listening** this is about making regular eye contact (not all the time, but a bit helps) and not doing other things at the same time (put your phone down!).

**Try not to judge** or jump to conclusions – this can push people to clam up again, and your assumptions may be wrong.

**Don't interrupt** it's annoying, and it suggests that you care more about what you have to say than listening to them.

**Try to resist offering solutions** or advice – especially if they're not being asked for. It's natural to want to help or to provide fixes, but sometimes people just want to get things off their chest.

**And show a little empathy**. Think about what it must be like to be in their shoes.

## Rate it

'On a scale of 1–10, how are you doing?' I've used this oh-so-simple question countless times to start a conversation with other men when they've found it tough. Try it for yourself.

# Part Four:

# Staying in the driving seat

Are there times when your emotions get the better of you? Do you find yourself getting wound up or feeling panicked in certain situations? In those moments, it can sometimes feel as if you're not in control of what you say or do (or don't say or do).

**The exercises and techniques in this section will help you get back some of that control.**

Some of them can be used right when you're heading towards those difficult times, so that you can get a handle on the situation and choose how you want to react. Others are there to help you recognize some of the patterns and triggers that lead up to them, again, giving you a chance to decide how you want to manage them.

Note that if you find yourself regularly struggling with these feelings, you don't have to deal with them on your own – it can be a good idea to chat to your doctor (see page 40).

# Take the edge off

These techniques are designed to help take the edge off when you need to calm down.

**Leave**

**1** Just taking a short walk can help you get some distance from the situation so you can think about it and decide how you want to respond. If you need to, tell people you could do with a breather.

**Breathe**

**2** Getting a handle on your breathing can help with managing difficult emotions in the moment. There's a simple breathing exercise on page 50 that you could try.

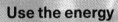

## Use the energy

**3**   Defuse your feelings in a way that doesn't hurt yourself or others. You could try hitting a punch bag, tearing up paper, sprinting fast or punching a pillow.

## Relax

**4**   If you can, try to release the tension by doing something relaxing. There's a muscle relaxation exercise coming up that can help and which involves tensing and relaxing all the main muscle groups.

6

# I'd had a panic attack before,

and I was sure it was happening again, but I just kept telling myself to breathe, over and over.

# I did the counting thing.

# And I did slowly feel more normal.

**Rav, 33, consultant**

# Breathe it out

This is a really simple one, but for some people it can be remarkably effective. The reason why it's so effective is that when you are experiencing heightened emotions it is reflected in your body, often by a higher pulse rate, tension in the muscles and more rapid breathing. You then sense that your body is in this tense mode and it heightens your emotions even further. But it can work in the other direction as well.

**If you can slow your pulse, ease your muscles and calm your breathing, you can also calm your emotions.**

The easiest way of doing this is by consciously changing your breathing. It also works in another way by diverting your mind and focusing it on simply taking air in and out of your lungs.

The next time you feel yourself heading into a difficult moment, find a quiet space and try this exercise.

**1** Sit or lie in a comfortable position.

**2** Breathe in slowly to the count of seven and breathe out slowly to the count of eleven.

**3** Repeat step 2 for as long as you need. A minute or two tends to be enough to make a difference.

**TIP:** If you can, breathe from the bottom of your lungs, using your diaphragm, rather than from the top of your lungs. This promotes deep breathing instead of shallow breathing. If you're doing it right, you'll notice that your belly starts going in and out.

# Relax

Before attempting this exercise, consider whether you have any injuries that might need managing, find a relaxing environment free from distractions, and don't do it after a big meal or after drinking alcohol. For each of the numbered steps in the sequence, follow this process:

 **Tense the muscle involved but not so much that you feel any pain.**

 **Hold the tension for about two seconds then relax the muscle for about five seconds.**

 **Sometimes saying the word 'relax' when releasing the muscle is helpful.**

 **When relaxed, let the muscle go limp and feel the weight in the muscle.**

## Now follow this sequence:

1. Right hand and forearm: make a fist with your right hand.

2. Right upper arm: bring your right forearm up to your shoulder to 'make a muscle'.

3. Left hand and forearm: make a fist with your left hand.

4. Left upper arm: bring your left forearm up to your shoulder to 'make a muscle'.

5. Forehead: raise your eyebrows as high as they will go, as though you were surprised by something.

6. Eyes and cheeks: squeeze your eyes tight shut.

7. Mouth and jaw: open your mouth as wide as you can, as you do when you're yawning.

8. Neck: face forward and then pull your head back slowly, as though you are looking up to the ceiling (be careful as you tense these muscles).

9. Shoulders: tense the muscles in your shoulders as you bring your shoulders up towards your ears.

10. Shoulder blades and back: push your shoulder blades back, trying to almost touch them together, so that your chest is pushed forward.

11. Chest and stomach: breathe in deeply, filling up your lungs and chest with air and then release.

12. Hips and buttocks: squeeze your buttock muscles.

13. Right upper leg: tighten your right thigh.

14. Right lower leg: pull your toes towards you to stretch the calf muscle (do this slowly and carefully to avoid cramps).

15. Left upper leg: tighten your left thigh.

16. Left lower leg: pull your toes towards you to stretch the calf muscle (do this slowly and carefully to avoid cramps).

**Practice means progress. Only through practice can you become more aware of your muscles, how they respond with tension, and how you can relax them. Training your body to respond differently to stress is like any training – practising consistently is the key.**

# Triggers

If you find yourself regularly struggling with your emotions, it might be worth thinking about patterns: when do certain emotions appear, what triggers them and how do you experience them?

For instance, there might be a link to a certain kind of interaction, work duty, social activity or day of the week. Do you find that a certain feeling hits with no warning or can you feel it coming on? How does it play out for you? When do things begin to ramp up, when do they cool down? And what is it actually like for you to go through? How does your body physically respond (sweaty palms, pulse racing, tension in your muscles, and so on)?

## What do you do next?

Once you have a sense of how things kick off, you are in a better position to decide what to do about it, interrupting your pattern before it gets going. You might find that it's helpful to deploy some of the methods in this book.

## Default reaction?

You might find that some of the feelings that are triggered in you are related more to your past than your present, and since then have become more like habits or default responses rather than feelings that are relevant to the here and now.

**If this is the case, it can be helpful to reflect on them and ask yourself if you could respond differently.**

# Part Five:

# Respect your life

**One of the most important truths I want to pass on is that you are the most important person in your life, and, if you don't know this already, know it now.**

Men often report seeing themselves as protectors or providers, but remember that you are not only valuable because you take care of other people. Although, if that idea helps you to take care of yourself, then great.

Maybe you don't need any convincing of this, in which case, don't let anyone shake you of that knowledge. But I often hear men who are in crisis say that they didn't seek help because they feel they should be able to handle their problems on their own; that they didn't want to take up their doctor's time or that they aren't worth the effort. Sadly, these beliefs are all too common, and they are simply not true.

——————

**No matter who you are, there will be difficulties in your life. Be sure that you respect them. Respect your part in dealing with them. And respect what you need in order to do that.**

——————

# The essentials

Life comes with its challenges and struggles, and in our modern world there are a truckload of new pressures that need negotiating. As a result, it's more important than ever that we take care of ourselves so that we can function efficiently. But not many of us actually do it. We're often too busy with other things, and taking care of yourself can amount to little more than slumping infront of the TV at the end of the day.

## Make time for yourself

Some small routines (that you might already be doing) are pretty effective at bringing calm to your day and impacting positively on your head space. Simple things like taking a coffee break, or a long shower, meeting up with friends – they can each have a surprisingly powerful effect on how we feel during the day.

There might also be other things that you used to do in the past, but that have slipped out from your routine, or that you would like to do but haven't got round to it. For example, I used to set my alarm an hour early and go for a short morning run, but then my daughter came along

and this practice soon stopped. I told myself at the time that I needed the extra sleep to cope with the demands of family life. But the truth is that keeping myself physically fit was a very important part of being able to manage my change in circumstances, and when I dropped that part of my routine I soon became lethargic, miserable and not myself. Maintaining that bit of time where I looked after myself, physically and mentally, was a great preparation for the day ahead and made me a fitter, happier father and husband.

# Spend some time thinking about what helps you function day-to-day.

These are things that you do on a daily, weekly, monthly or yearly basis. Appreciate how doing these things changes how you feel.

# Get some space

Call it a 'man cave', call it a shed, call it your bedroom, call it the park. The name doesn't matter, as long as you have one: a space where you can chill out and just be you, for a couple of hours – or even just half an hour – at a time.

When I say 'space' I'm really talking about head space. Putting on some headphones for a period of time and shutting out external sounds could suffice, if that's what relaxes you and takes you out of everyday life for a bit.

Just to be clear, in case you're starting to feel as if I'm expecting you to go off and have some profound experience, I'm not suggesting you need to spend that time in deep contemplation of your psyche.

## Do what you want, what you enjoy.

There are a couple of exercises later in this book (see 'The pursuit of happiness' on page 98) that could come in handy here. Feel free to stare into space if you want to.

Time out is the essential
thing, so get outside,
go for a walk or a run,
lie back with some music,
read a book – give yourself
that time.

# Managing your time

Knowing the importance of having 'space' that is just yours is a start. Now you have to make sure that you actually do something about it.

Time is one of those things that we never seem to have enough of. But we all make decisions about how we spend it and what we prioritize. Given that your head space influences how you experience your life, taking care of it should be right at the top of that list. Coffee breaks, hitting the gym, crosswords, whatever it is that makes a difference, these are the non-negotiables. They might not feel like it right now, but they are.

## Making them a regular part of your life is key.

Many of them probably already are, but if not, try scheduling them in your diary. Make them a regular (weekly) thing, so that Tuesday nights become the night that you go to kick-boxing, book club or whatever.

Are there things on your list that you can do with other people? Making a plan with someone else can be another way of helping make sure that you stick to it.

## Reminders

Putting a reminder in your phone can help make sure you do the little things as well as the big things. For example, if you work at a desk you could set a reminder to make sure you take breaks to get up and walk about a bit, maybe look out of a window, stretch your back out.

# Part Six:

# Lifestyle

In the spirit of leading by example, first I had to ask myself how I would describe my lifestyle. Do I even have a lifestyle? I wish I had a few pithy words to sum up what my life looked like on the outside. I don't. But it is something we all have to think about, because how you live is significant, especially if some elements of your lifestyle are holding you back, or affecting your self-esteem and confidence, or are just plain bad for you.

A good place to start is to think about what mindsets mark your daily life. For instance, I would probably describe myself as someone who is undisciplined, slow off the mark, hesitant, impatient, argumentative, selective and pushy (as well as kind, considerate, chatty, friendly, sporty, funny, smart, modern and good-looking!).

———

**It's also important to think about how these mindsets affect you and those around you and what habits they lead to.**

———

No habit has to be inherently good or bad, but if we don't take the time to think about how our habits are affecting us, we can be living a life that we haven't chosen. I know that some of my habits are ones that I've just sort of slipped into – smoking, for instance. One day on the bus on the way home from school, my friends and I found a packet of cigarettes, lit up and smoked. I just kept it up until I realized that I didn't actually want to smoke, and I knew it was only doing me damage. When I gave it up, I decided I'd have tea breaks instead of cigarette breaks. As I say, few habits are all bad or all good. But if you can work out the different ways in which they affect you, then you can make choices about them, keeping the helpful stuff and reducing the unhelpful.

# Habits of choice

Have a look at the page opposite and locate all of the words or expressions that apply to you. This certainly isn't an exhaustive list, so think about what's missing as well. For each of the things that you come up with, ask yourself the following questions:

**How does it impact my life?**

**What do I get out of it?**

**Is it helping (and how) or not (and how)?**

**Do I want to change it?**

Remember, these things might not be inherently good or bad. For instance, exercising is generally seen as a good thing, but if you're doing it to excess then it probably isn't helping. Being conscious about how and why you live your life the way you do can not only deepen your understanding of yourself, it can also help you to take control and make decisions about what you want your life to be like.

If you want to reduce or stop any of these habits, but feel that it'll be tough on your own, there are people out there who will give you guidance and support.

# 'I think things through'

I exercise
I game
I smoke
I party
I overeat
I under-eat
I take drugs
I read
I have sex
I volunteer
I hike
I gamble
I make money
I write poetry
I garden
I work hard
I play hard
I take early morning
  cold showers
I go to bed early
I am early to rise
I plan out each day
I keep a journal

I surround myself
  with positive people
I believe in lifelong
  learning
I trust my intuition
I give thanks
I meditate
I take a fifteen-minute
  walk every single day
I am tolerant
I mentor
I have a dog
I cycle to work
I gave up smoking
I cut down on alcohol
I feel I'm not enough
  on my own
I spend time with my
  parents
I don't eat meat
I drive everywhere
I recycle
I respect women

# Connect

Humans are social animals – we are primed to connect with the people around us. Strengthening our relationships, whatever they are, is good for our physical and mental health – and it's not just beneficial for us as individuals, but for others, too. Strong, supportive social networks are a win-win.

Different people benefit from different kinds and quantities of relationships so there's no prescription here. But give it some attention. Are there things that you could do to strengthen and broaden your relationships?

## You could consider:

1. Preparing a meal with someone

2. Phoning people rather than texting or emailing, or if they're far away, try Skype/video chat

3. Arranging a day out to somewhere unusual, with friends or family

4. Going out for lunch with a colleague

5. Becoming a mentor at work

6. Rather than just nodding to your neighbour, asking them how they're doing

7. Volunteering at a local hospital, charity or community group

8. Joining a club or team, or starting a course

9. Supporting your local sports team

10. Visiting your local church, mosque, synagogue, gurdwara or other place of faith

# Devices

On average we spend over four hours a day on our phones, and that's not including when we switch to tablets and computers. Using tech has become an integral part of most people's lifestyle. And it needs some thought. And action.

Just like with our habits, our devices aren't inherently bad or good; in fact, they have made a significant difference to our lives, and mainly for the common good, if used in a balanced way.

## What I am concerned with here is the importance of knowing how the use of devices affects you.

Break down what you actually do on your phone, and how much you do it. Do you send the odd text, make only necessary phone calls, check your emails from time to time – and log on to social media once or twice a day, maximum? Or is your screen time more intensive? How about your tablet? Your computer? How much time on average do you spend on each? How do each of these activities affect you? Is your phone always on? Is it always with you?

## Set your boundaries

Your answers might sit comfortably in your life, but if not then it's time to think about setting boundaries around your use of devices. There's no hard and fast rules here – limiting your time on Twitter to ten minutes a day isn't going to be practical if you use it for work, and I know I laughed the first time my games console told me to take a break and go outside. But think about what feels right for you and at what point going online feels 'gratuitous' – meaning you aren't doing it for any other reason than boredom or habit. Setting boundaries can be as simple as turning off notifications, moving certain apps (like your work email) off your home screen so you don't feel tempted to check it on the weekend. Also, turning it off at night-time, not using it for your morning alarm, limiting some apps to certain times of the day. I recently decided that I wouldn't look at Facebook in the morning because once I did, I would check one status update after another, then view a couple of videos, read a news report (and then feel compelled to comment on it).

My time on social media was eating into my work time and activities, and it didn't make me feel good.

Swapping negative habits (e.g. scrolling through photos of artificial 'perfect' lives) for positive habits (e.g. listening to an audiobook) is a helpful switch; it reduces anxiety and feelings of inadequacy. Keep an eye on your device use, and if you feel that you're slipping back into ways that bring you stress or anxiety, try again (for tips on how to change your habits, look at 'Make it a Habit' on page 82).

## Social media

In terms of mental health and tech, social media is the thing that seems to hit the headlines the most. For many people it doesn't cause a problem, but for others a drip-feed of carefully selected and edited pictures is a sure-fire route to low self-esteem.

**Maybe you're not ready to delete Instagram and cull your Facebook friends, but if this is an issue for you be sure that you do something.**

"For many people, the drip-feed

**of carefully selected and edited pictures**

is a sure-fire route to low self-esteem."

# Respect sleep

You might be thinking that sleep isn't really a lifestyle choice, it's just something that you do for a bit during every twenty-four-hour period, but respecting your need to sleep is vital. We spend about one-third of our lives sleeping and good-quality sleep helps everything from physical health to mental cognition, to emotional health.

Not surprisingly, most of us don't feel we get enough of it. Depending on your lifestyle – staying out till the early hours too many nights a week, working overtime, eating late at night, having a young family – you could be losing out on the sleep you need (eight hours, ideally). Importantly, your state of mind affects your sleep, too; the stresses of life, anxiety and depression – they'll keep you awake at night.

Often the extent of dealing with it involves swallowing a double-shot espresso or an energy drink or supplement in the morning. But this doesn't solve the problem and can even make it worse. If you're regularly feeling tired, a bit on the edge, there are things you can do to change that, and to help you get enough good-quality sleep at night.

## Tips for sleep

If you struggle to prioritize sleep, you could try these tips.

**Establish a routine** by going to bed and waking at roughly the same time every day, even at the weekends. Consistency is good for your body clock and the brain will start to know when it's time to go to sleep.

**Avoid anything stimulating** (physically or mentally) an hour before you go to bed. This should be 'wind down time'.

**Avoid eating** – especially rich food – at least two hours before you go to bed.

**Check in with yourself** about any stress or anxiety you're feeling. Issues at work or in relationships, grief and loss, money problems – what's going on in our waking lives can keep us awake at night.

**Reduce nicotine and caffeine,** which are both stimulants and can interfere with getting to sleep. Avoid 4–6 hours before going to bed.

**Avoid screens** for an hour or so before going to bed, as the bright light has been shown to negatively affect sleep.

# Part Seven:

# Physical health

You can't really split up mental health and physical health: if you're taking care of one, you're helping the other.

In general, men find it easier to take care of their physical health than their mental health; although that's not always the case. For example, despite prostate cancer going hugely underdiagnosed, cancer charities are still having difficulty persuading enough men to get themselves checked out. The same goes for testicular cancer, too. Regular checking can save your life.

Living with a chronic illness or physical problem often has an impact on mental health, and it's important to consider that impact and what support you might need. But in general, in terms of what you can do to help yourself, you know it already: don't smoke, manage any alcohol and drug consumption, take regular exercise and try to eat well. It's not as easy as it sounds, and I'm not a magician, so I can't prescribe the perfect diet to knock depression on the head, for example, because that diet doesn't exist. But thinking about what you eat can help.

## Maintain a good balance of enjoying your life and looking after yourself.

It's up to you to decide how you want to manage your physical health. Just know that it's important that you do, to whatever degree feels healthy and sustainable to you.

# Small wins

When you want to make lasting changes, it helps to keep them manageable. So, we're not talking about taking on an iron-man regime or getting ready for a marathon (but if that's your thing, knock yourself out). Every small change you make that improves your diet or increases the amount of exercise that you get makes a difference. And you're far more likely to succeed if you keep it realistic.

> **Working out what is most doable with your lifestyle can make the difference between you sticking to it and not.**

Can you manage eating five servings of vegetables and fruit per day? Do it. Can you park the car a mile away from your destination and walk the rest? Do it. Can you regularly visit the gym that you're paying a subscription for? Do it. Go for a swim, jog or cycle, or play golf, tennis, or basketball with your friends, or even visit a steam room or sauna (these last two may not raise the heart rate but they're still good for your head space).

If you can't easily make it to the gym, could you walk home from work? If preparing a fresh meal every night is never going to happen, could you make a batch of something on the weekend and freeze it, or are there healthier take-out options you could choose?

**Remember, you don't have to change everything at once. It's better to choose one thing and stick to it.**

# When I find my work getting on top of me, I head to the gym or my local swimming pool.

# It allows me to focus my mind on something else entirely, and I return to work calmer and feeling more able to deal with things.

**Simon, 38, journalist**

# Make it a habit

One of the best ways of sustaining lifestyle changes is to make them a habit. Consider for a minute that much of the caretaking that you now do regularly has happened over time. Maybe you never flossed your teeth every night before ten years ago, but now you do. Before kids, you didn't do the school run every day, but you don't even think about it now. There was a time when you couldn't imagine doing these things every day, but now they're just part of your life. If you're making a choice, then stick to it, so it is no longer a choice, it is a given.

The first step is to pick one thing and make sure that it's manageable (see the previous exercise). You could then try some of the following tips to have a better chance of success:

## 1 Thirty days, minimum

Whatever you decide to do, try to keep to it for at least thirty days. Put the effort and energy in for one month, and it'll become easier to maintain afterwards.

## 2 Connect your new habit to an established habit

For example, when you hang your jacket up after work, also pick up your trainers; when you go shopping for veg, pick up one more item, too.

## 3 Involve someone else

Whether it's posting about your progress on social media, or playing squash with a friend, or just telling your family that you're going to have a smoothie every morning.

## 4 Reward yourself

Especially during those first thirty days. It needn't be something big. Go to the barber and get a hot-towel shave. Treat yourself to a massage (seriously, not enough men do this and that is a crying shame – a good muscle kneading changes lives!). Go to the theatre/cinema/ bowling alley or out with your mates. Check out the first episode of that box set you've been meaning to see but have been too busy to watch.

—————

# Failure is not failure

As a kid, I wish I'd known then what I know now about failure. If I did, I would not have felt so terrible when I failed all my school exams. My world had caved in, and I thought that I was not worthy of anything good in my life.

After several more attempts (and failures) I know now that failure is actually a good thing. Without it, we wouldn't strengthen, improve and succeed. We need to fail and make mistakes.

## The key is not to see it as the end point but as a learning point.

Lincoln wouldn't have been president without several failed runs and Bill Gates wouldn't have established Microsoft without first developing the abortive Traf-O-Data.

There is no sports team that has won a game, match or tournament without analysing the games they lost. And my daughter would never have learned to ride her bike if she wasn't prepared to fall off it at least once!

This idea applies to most things in life, and can be particularly helpful for when you're making changes. If you lose, or make a mistake one time, don't dwell on it, instead, think about what you'd like to do differently another time, learn from the experience and move forward.

Failure is something you can improve on; make it your aim to fail better. For instance, if you've tried a change that you thought was manageable but actually isn't, what was it that stopped you? What can you change to make it more doable? Is there an alternative? Just because you thought that playing squash every week would be the answer doesn't mean it'll end up that way. If you haven't done it before, how would you even know?

And equally, if you do start to notice a change becoming a habit, that's an achievement worth recognizing. Is there anything that you could learn from the success? Why did this one stick and not others?

## As you learn what doesn't work, you'll get better at getting better.

# Part Eight:

# Work

Though not all work involves earning money – childcare, homemaking, volunteering etc. – *all* kinds of work involve making a contribution of time and effort, and work is predominantly good for us. Whether you are sitting behind a desk, managing a building site, regularly standing up in court to defend a client, or working shifts in a hospital or a factory, whatever you do for work can be instrumental in raising and maintaining your self-esteem and increasing your sense of purpose and satisfaction in life.

Contributing to the world we live in makes us feel useful and part of a wider community. For some of us, work is the most important part of our lives. For me, as old school as it sounds, working and partaking in meaningful work is one of those things that lie at the core of my identity.

Of course, work can sometimes feel like a burden, and it can come at the expense of a balanced life. And though attitudes are changing, for men, the pressure to prioritize work over everything else – to bring home the bacon, to be a 'provider'– can be overwhelming. For many of us, that leads to stress, anxiety and sometimes even burnout. It can be hard to push back against that pressure, but there are things that you can do to make the stress of it manageable.

## Disclaimer

I need to put my hands up and say that I really struggle to keep boundaries around work. I've often failed to keep to the advice that I give out. But the more I try, the more it sticks. And I know it's worth it, because when I'm successful at maintaining a balance, I really see the difference in me and in those around me.

# Balance and boundaries

What part does work play in your life? It might be that you've struck a comfortable work-life balance, but for more and more of us our jobs encroach on other areas. The once standard nine to five regime is now more of a fond memory than a reality; and with our phones in our pockets many of us have become twenty-four-hour workers, whether we realize it or not. Whatever your situation, consider what balance you currently have and how it affects you. If that balance is off, creating boundaries might help slide the scale back.

What those boundaries are likely to be depends on the kind of work that you do. Some of the suggestions below won't fit with your situation, but it's worth considering each category in case you can make changes that are better suited to your lifestyle:

**Regular breaks:** schedule them, give them a focus, but most of all take them!

**Lunch:** this needs its own category because lunch (or whatever main meal(s) occur while you're working) deserves your respect. Take a proper lunch break, where you stop working (full stop). If you can, leave your work space, go for a walk, or consider eating lunch with colleagues or a friend.

**Working hours:** be clear on your working hours and stick to them, which means getting to and leaving work on time. Once you've left for the day, try not to check in again until you're back the next morning: no looking at or responding to work emails; no fitting in a little something extra while you're on the couch. If you work at home, the same applies; even if your hours are not nine to five, make the distinction between work and play. This discipline can be difficult to establish as you may feel pressure to be 'on call' for your clients or employers, but switching off and properly occupying your downtime provides real benefits.

**Work space:** if you do work for yourself and don't have an office away from home, then try to make sure you have a distinct work space, ideally a separate room or study, but if not, a corner of another room in your home. Don't occupy this space when you've finished working. Turn off your computer and any lighting there.

**Mark the end of the working day:** even when you leave work, it's easy for your mind to keep whirring around the problems of the day and sometimes it isn't possible to shut them out, but try. Doing something that really marks the transition out of work, such as reading a book on the journey home, having a cup of something when you get in, or scheduling an after-work activity, really helps take your mind off work.

**Holidays:** take them. If you have a holiday allowance, use all of it. If you work for yourself, budget and plan for time off.

**Parental leave:** be aware of your rights and what choices are available. Don't just follow the herd.

## Change expectations

Implementing these changes can be difficult at first, so build them up slowly and start to re-educate your colleagues in terms of their expectations. For example: if you stop replying to emails on weekends, people will be more likely to stop having this expectation of you. If you work in a team of people, you can also start changing the broader culture, helping others with their own balance. Notice how implementing these changes positively improves your working and your head space.

# Even if your hours are not nine to five, make the distinction between work and play.

(Switching off and properly occupying your downtime provides real benefits.)

# Taking care of yourself at work

When I got myself a smartwatch I downloaded an app that reminded me to take regular breaks at work: to breathe and to relax. It has made a huge difference. I feel more productive, calm and connected to whatever it is that I'm doing. These days I'm proud to confess that birdsong tracks make up my daily playlist. (I'd like to point out that gone are the days of panpipes and whale song; the natural soundscapes you can get with streaming services and apps is just like being out on a mountainside or in the middle of the Amazon, and who wouldn't want that?!)

So, along with addressing your work-life balance, there are other things you can do to make your job less stressful and generally more pleasant. Here are some ideas:

**To-do lists:** make a list of what needs to be done and then as you complete each task cross it off. And if you do extra tasks in between, write them down on the list and cross each of them out, too. Remember to keep the timescales small; think in terms of a week, day or even morning.

**Be realistic:** I'm one of those optimists who assume they can steamroller through mountains of work at a breakneck pace every day. I'm wrong. I can't. When you're thinking about your to-do lists try to be realistic, because priorities can and do change.

**Reflect:** at the end of each day look back at that list and take a moment to appreciate what you've achieved. If there are things that you haven't crossed off, think about why that is. Were you being too ambitious? Did you have an unusual number of distractions that day? Don't leave those things on the old list, but when you start the next day, copy them out again so you can approach them afresh.

**Your environment:** could you personalize your space? Rearrange it to make it easier to work with? Is your chair comfortable? Is the light adequate? Clearing the clutter and making sure your working conditions are right is often a good place to start.

**Take a breath:** if you find the stress mounting, take a minute to breathe deeply. (See page 50 for a breathing technique you can use.)

## Networking

If you are self-employed and don't have many, or any, colleagues to either contend with or bounce ideas and issues off, make an effort to network with other self-employed workers. These people don't even have to be in the same industry or area of work as you, but they may provide inspiration, advice or tips; or they may just be company. Working for yourself has much to be said for it, but it can be isolating. Get out there and network with like-minded workers.

**Ask for help:** from your manager, colleagues, friends, family, whoever. If you need to talk about changes to the way you work or delegating tasks, having a strong support network of people to talk to or to lean on is worth its weight in gold.

## Give your breaks a focus

**Get outside (or inside):** whichever environment you're in, change it. Go for a walk outside or have a sit down inside.

**Stretch:** think about your back, your neck, your shoulders, your jaw. Focus on the parts of your body that have been taking the strain and stretch them out.

**Music:** listen to songs that you really enjoy and let them fill up your mind.

**Chat:** make someone a cup of coffee and hang around for a few minutes to chat while they take the first few sips.

# Lifelong learning

When you think about your future does learning feature? As we get older, we tend to learn less. It's just the way things are set up. We go to school, stuff things into our brains for a bit and then we're unleashed on the world. Learning done.

Of course, that's not true for everyone, and most people pick up new skills via their jobs or hobbies, but we don't tend to devote the same kind of time or attention to it as we did when we were kids. That's something to think about, because just the act of regular learning can boost self-confidence and self-esteem, help build a sense of purpose, as well as connecting us with others.

And to be clear, learning doesn't have to mean taking up a formal course. It doesn't have to be about brain training and building a more agile mind. It's much more about curiosity and discovering new things.

**It might be learning to fix your bike or trying out a new recipe.**

It might be learning a new language, or taking on a new duty at work. If you find something interesting, could you look into it more? YouTube is packed with tutorials, and there are lots of apps aimed at teaching new skills. And if you get a taste for something then you could take it up a step and look into going on a course and getting a qualification.

## Set your own goals, modest or large. Even just reading this book counts.

# Part Nine:

# The pursuit of happiness

No one can be 'happy' all of the time. It doesn't matter what it looks like on Facebook or Instagram, they just aren't. Humans aren't meant to be. And quite frankly, we'd be pretty irritating if we were.

The definition of happiness has been debated endlessly over the centuries; no one really knows what it means. But constantly chasing it is pointless. Happiness can mean a fleeting moment of euphoria, and it can mean a more lasting feeling of contentment and being at peace with yourself and your life. Happiness is sometimes so ordinary that you don't even notice it. These days it's confusing – social media is pedalling us an impossible ideal when it comes to how we should be looking or living or feeling or behaving. Online, everything seems to be either great (look at my perfect life/kids/partner/job/holiday), or terrible (look at the state of the world). There are many other ways of being and feeling and they're all OK and normal.

## In fact, the best path to happiness is to stop worrying that there's something wrong with the way you are.

We can be content, thoughtful, calm, safe, solid, cool, fine, on a level, as well as being ecstatic, or frustrated, anxious, upset, angry or down. That's how it is. Of course, if you're struggling with negative feelings then you should pay attention to that, but otherwise, try to aim for being generally content with yourself and how you see your world. Happiness means different things to all of us – try not to measure yours against others people's.

That said, feeling good is a key part of well-being, and working towards recognizing the positive in your life and increasing it is always a good thing.

# Take stock

It seems to be a whole lot easier to concentrate on the things that we don't have than on the things that we do. Taking stock of what you do have in your life often needs a mental effort (I don't know anyone who kicks off their day listing all the wonderful things in their life) but learning to be grateful pays dividends, not least because it allows you to celebrate the good that you have right now, promoting optimism and fostering positivity.

**Think now about what you are grateful for. It might only feel like small things but it all adds up.**

Is there a way that you can remind yourself of these things more often? For instance, you could keep a photograph of loved ones on your desk or in your wallet or as your phone background. Or a memento hanging from your car's rear-view mirror. Or a note on your front door to remind yourself every time you leave your home. Even a ringtone that reminds you of someone or a time in your life that was special.

**Keep the good stuff close.**

# I've got a picture of my family on my keyring.

## It was taken when we were on a roller coaster and we're all upside-down.

# I don't always notice it, but sometimes it'll catch my eye and it makes me smile.

**Tony, 45, gardener**

# What *really* makes you happy?

We're told that a lot of things should make us happy (most of them involve buying stuff). We know by now that it doesn't work like that. Something that one person enjoys another will hate. Someone once told me that it took them until their thirties to be able to say that they hated clubbing. Their friends loved it, and he was supposed to love it too, so he sacrificed most of his Saturday nights to sweaty, deafening rooms, when all he wanted was to be in the pub. It just seemed easier somehow to go along with it. But it was a waste. And it took him thinking hard about what he really wanted to do – not what others wanted him to do or what he thought he ought to want to do – to get his Saturday nights back.

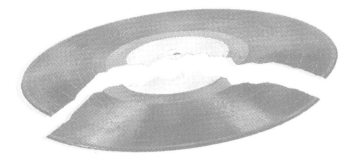

What do you enjoy? It's not just about things that keep you going but things you love to do – big or small – that bring a smile to your face.

## Keep in mind that what we enjoy changes over time. Stuff you loved when you were younger might not be the same now.

Or perhaps there are things that you used to do that have just slipped away.

### Schedule it in

Once again, knowing about what makes us feel good is one thing, making sure that we do it is another. Prioritize your good times. Think about each of the things on your list. When can you next do them? Make a plan. Could any of them become regular parts of your day/week/month/year?

# Play time

You used to do it when you were a kid, but then you got older and just having fun for fun's sake seemed to be less and less a part of life. I'm talking about stuff that doesn't necessarily get you anywhere: it's not constructive, it won't get you a promotion, doesn't make you a better person, or cleverer, or fitter.

## You might see it as a waste of time. But you enjoy doing it.

Maybe you've already got a few of these things on your list from the previous exercise, but if you don't, it might be worth adding one or two in.

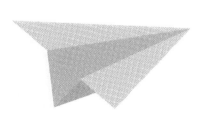

It could be something like watching repeats of your favourite film, messing about with your pet, reminiscing with a loved one, playing video games (not excessively), making a high tower of all those saved coins, building paper planes and launching them off the highest building you can find, creating a BIG Lego house.

Naturally, balance is the key here. It's not going to help your feeling of well-being and happiness to do these things all the time, but giving yourself permission just to have fun once in a while is not only not a bad idea, it's good for you.

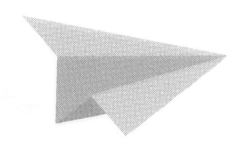

# Part Ten:

# Bad times

Life isn't always rosy; we will all come up against difficult and painful times. Though you can't avoid them, the good news is that you *can* equip yourself to get through them.

**It's during the bad times that we dig deep and use all our resources to cope with what's coming at us.**

Knowing yourself well (see page 12) is a key part of navigating life's bumps in the road – whether it's how well you engage with your emotions or knowing what helps to reinforce your natural resilience.

We've all got inbuilt resilience, that ability to bounce back and adapt in the face of challenging times, and there are things that you can do to strengthen it.

> **'Bad times have a scientific value. These are occasions a good learner would not miss.'**
>
> **Ralph Waldo Emerson**

# Bouncing back

This probably isn't your first knock, so use what you've learned from your experiences. Looking back on tough times that you've coped with and survived is a valuable reminder that things can and will change, that you will get through this event and, importantly, that you will learn from it.

Think about how you coped back then. What did you learn from how you responded? What helped and how? How did you take care of yourself? What would you do differently next time? My own favourite antidote is brilliantly expressed by Matt Haig in his book *Reasons to Stay Alive*: 'Love is anxiety's greatest killer. Love is an outward force. It's our road out of our own terrors, because anxiety is an illness that wraps us up in our own nightmares. Having people who love you and that you love is such a help. This doesn't have to be romantic, or even familial love. Forcing yourself to see the world through love's gaze can be healthy. Love is an attitude to life. It can save us.'

## Bad times in the past

Some difficult experiences are not easy to get over, even if you survived them at the time. Sometimes they can stick with you, even hinder your progress through life.

It might be that doing some of the exercises in this book have brought those tough experiences into focus again. This is not uncommon and it isn't a bad thing – facing up to your 'demons' is healthy – but depending on how negatively they are affecting you, it can be a good idea to seek help, either from your doctor or a counsellor.

# Resilience toolkit

We have the power to change our resilience, and taking a proactive approach will mean you're ready when you need to be. When you're thinking about bolstering your resilience, keep in mind these three key areas: mental state, social connections and ways of coping. Building each one will build your resilience, and most of the exercises in this book are designed to help you do just that.

When your mood drops it can take your energy and motivation with it, so it's a good idea to have solid 'mental equipment' and coping methods ready to help you during such times. You could look back to 'The essentials' and 'What *really* makes you happy'. Are there things that you came up with there that you could use when you're struggling? Keep a list on your phone (or wherever is easily accessible) and add to it whenever you notice something (or someone) that's boosted your mood. Think of it as your own personal resilience toolkit.

TIP: Having things physically to hand that you can quickly turn to also makes a difference. Whether that's a playlist on your phone, your favourite book in a drawer at home or work, or a photo from your last holiday as your screensaver. Mementos and reminders of good conversations and good times, of loved ones, friends, pets etc. – these are valuable parts of your resilience toolkit and represent a positive and proactive approach towards good well-being.

Stephen King novels. I guess it sounds like a weird choice if you're feeling bad, but it works for me.

Dan, 22, dog-walker

# Part Eleven:

# Purpose

I have always seen my purpose in life as contributing something useful and sustainable to my immediate community. It's pretty clear where this came from. Born in London to a family of immigrants with few connections, I very quickly realized that we were poor and that we depended on each other to survive in what was for most of the time a harsh and unwelcoming world. Sacrifices were made by all and for the benefit of others. We would never have survived if it wasn't for that.

Living with adversity soon taught me that it was only through having a sense of purpose that I could then develop the intention, the drive and the motivation to live in the way that I wanted to. Purpose takes you a long way along the journey of overcoming life's challenges and becoming the real you.

When I talk about 'purpose', I don't mean it in the sense of what you were put on this earth to do – although feel free to look at it like that if you want to. Instead, it's about discovering what your values are. Values are attitudes, beliefs and behaviour that you feel strongly matter to you and that may have been influenced by your upbringing, parents and carers, your faith, cultural background, school, peers, the media and so on.

> **'The two most important days in your life are the day you were born and the day you find out why.'**
>
> **Mark Twain**

# Values

Most of the time, your goals will line up with your values. For instance, one life goal I have is to actively avoid going along with friends with whom I disagree. I was brought up to always work hard and behave well at school, regardless of what my friends might have thought. As boring as it may have seemed at the time, it got me out of a few scrapes, that's for sure.

On the opposite page is a list of common values. Do any of these motivate and inspire you? If not, what does? Keep in mind that they might not be the same ones that motivated and inspired you five years ago, as values can and do change over time.

How do your life goals sit with them? If there is a difference between what you want to achieve in life and what you value then you might want to think about where that goal came from.

## Are you carrying someone else's values/goals?

- [ ] respect
- [ ] friendship
- [ ] stability
- [ ] reliability
- [ ] fun
- [ ] independence
- [ ] assertiveness
- [ ] humility
- [ ] money
- [ ] power
- [ ] acceptance
- [ ] patience
- [ ] gratitude
- [ ] love
- [ ] honesty
- [ ] sustainability
- [ ] kindness
- [ ] trust
- [ ] justice
- [ ] intimacy
- [ ] spirituality
- [ ] community
- [ ] open-mindedness
- [ ] equality
- [ ] ambition
- [ ] bravery
- [ ] hope
- [ ] responsibility
- [ ] integrity
- [ ] fairness

- [ ] self-respect
- [ ] accomplishment
- [ ] safety
- [ ] awareness
- [ ] commitment
- [ ] compassion
- [ ] dependability
- [ ] empathy
- [ ] balance
- [ ] growth
- [ ] hard work
- [ ] health
- [ ] comfort
- [ ] truth
- [ ] motivation
- [ ] openness
- [ ] optimism
- [ ] passion
- [ ] productivity
- [ ] purpose
- [ ] possibility
- [ ] self-reliance
- [ ] sensitivity
- [ ] serenity
- [ ] service
- [ ] sharing
- [ ] simplicity
- [ ] sincerity
- [ ] support
- [ ] imagination

# Achievable goals

The goals we pursue, whether big or small, are often not easy to accomplish. If they were, we'd be doing them all already. Taking stock of how pursuing certain goals impacts you in terms of stress is important as you consider how you manage reaching them and what balance you want to achieve in your life.

## The purpose of this exercise is to help you get that perspective.

First, think about your goals for the year ahead and list them in a table like the one opposite (this one has been filled out as a demonstration). Next, rate each of them, from 1 to 10, on how important they are to you. And then again on how stressful they are. Spend some time doing this. You might notice that you change your scores as you compare different goals to one another.

Next, plot your responses on a graph like the one over the page, which has been filled out with the scores from the demonstration table. The intention here is to provide a snapshot of how pursuing your goals impacts you in terms of stress.

| Goal number | Goal description | Importance* | Stress inducing* |
|---|---|---|---|
| 1 | Spend more time with family | 8 | 6 |
| 2 | Start a new training course | 3 | 7 |
| 3 | End an acrimonious relationship | 8 | 10 |
| 4 | Get a new job | 6 | 8 |
| 5 | Regularly exercise | 5 | 5 |
| 6 | Buy a new car | 2 | 4 |
| 7 | Meditate daily | 6 | 1 |
| 8 | Sleep for a minimum of seven hours | 8 | 3 |

* Importance and Stress inducing ranked from 1 (least) to 10 (most)

As you'll see, the graph is colour-coded to help you focus on certain areas.

**White:** low stress, high pay-off – go for it!

**Yellow:** not a high priority but also not too taxing – carry on.

**Orange:** matters the most but high stress – consider stress management.

**Red:** high stress, low pay-off – consider ditching.

Your first job is to establish which goals you take forward and which goals you let go (either temporarily for the year or permanently). It might be that all your goals are safely out of the high stress areas, but if you have a few floating around the red, or many of them bunched up around the orange, it is sensible to consider whether you can tolerate that amount of stress.

When I did this exercise recently, I decided to put aside my goal of taking on the PhD I'd been planning on starting for years. When I saw it on the graph in the context of what I wanted to achieve with my life and what mattered to me, I could feel how it just wasn't as relevant as it had been – nor worth the stress! Letting it go was a relief. I hadn't realized how stressful it was to have had it hanging over me. A few months on I can tell that I feel far more positive in general. I might start a PhD at some point, but I suspect that I won't, and I'm happy with that.

For those goals that you decide to take forward, make a plan for how you will achieve them and how you will manage the accompanying stress. The following exercise gives some advice.

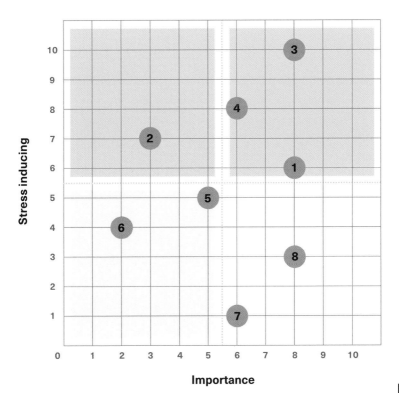

# Make a plan

How you work out how to achieve your goals is up to you, but a good principle with any challenge is to break it down into manageable chunks. Then, for each chunk, set a timescale of when you expect to be able to start it and when you will have it completed. Be realistic, and don't worry if you miss the deadline (life has a habit of getting in the way), but do set a new deadline to aim for (see page 62 for more ideas on this).

For how you manage any accompanying stress, look back to the exercises in 'Respect your life' on page 56 for ideas on what you might need. It's also worth thinking about how you will assess whether these measures are working. The exercise 'Ask yourself' on page 38 can be useful here.

If you find that your stress levels are becoming a problem for you, consider what support network you have to help you with this: friends, family or colleagues? Are there other responsibilities that you could put to one side while you focus on achieving your goal? Could you split the chunks up further so that they're more manageable? Do you need to take a break? Remember, your mental state is always a priority and taking care of it will also ultimately make you better able to achieve your goals.

## Self-belief

To put it simply, nothing can be achieved without belief. If you believe you can't do it, you'll soon find out that you are right. But with belief in your self, there is potential, possibility and purpose.

# Self-belief is a powerful, motivating and enabling force.

Project out to the world what you want to get back from it. Have confidence in what you want to achieve, and no matter who you are or where you started from, you are giving yourself the very best chance.

# Resources

For further information and support on taking care of your head space, you can contact the Mind Infoline.

**Phone: 0300 123 3393**
**Text: 86463**
**Monday to Friday, 9am to 6pm (except for bank holidays).**
**Or email: info@mind.org.uk**

You can find additional resources on the Mind website at **mind.org.uk**

For support and advice in your area, find your local Mind at **mind.org.uk/localmind**

For advice on talking to your doctor, check out Mind's 'Find the Words' campaign: **mind.org.uk/findthewords**

If you are feeling overwhelmed or need a listening ear, we recommend contacting Samaritans.

**Phone: 116 123**
**24 hours a day, 365 days a year**

The charity CALM (Campaign Against Living Miserably) also offers a webchat service and helpline.

**Phone (nationwide): 0800 58 58 58**
**Phone (London): 0808 802 58 58**
**5pm to midnight, 365 days a year**

**mentalhealth.org.uk** is dedicated to finding and addressing the sources of mental health problems. They have lots of useful information and resources for taking care of your own mental health.

The **mankindproject.org** is a global men's network that focuses on bringing men together to work on shared projects and missions and to support one another throughout their lives.

The **mensadviceline.org.uk** offers a confidential helpline for all men (whether in heterosexual or same-sex relationships) experiencing domestic violence by a current or ex-partner.

**Phone: 0808 801 0327**
**Monday to Friday, 9am to 5pm**

**Rotimi Akinsete** is a therapeutic counsellor and clinical supervisor with extensive experience in community and NHS counselling services. He is currently the Director of Wellbeing at the University of Surrey and is also the founder and director of Black Men on the Couch, a special interest project focusing on psychotherapy and identity politics of African and Caribbean men and boys.

He has worked as an independent facilitator, trainer and advisor on various transformational leadership programmes and has sat on a number of panels and workshops around the subject of counselling and psychotherapy.

© Paul Stead Photography